TWISTED LIES 2

SEDONA VENEZ

"Oh, what a tangled web we weave. When first we practice to deceive!"
—**Sir Walter Scott**

❧ I ❧

CORE

I ABSENTLY TRACED the scar across my brow while staring at the Manhattan skyline. Mom's killer was New York City's mayoral hopeful Bigsby Calhoune—and I wanted him dead.

But killing him fast would be too easy. I planned to ruin him, stripping away everything he held dear—his wealth, his trophy fiancée Cate, his political career, and his freedom.

Bigsby was a dirty criminal underneath his slick, cleaned-up politician veneer. He might have a new identity and lifestyle, but he was still the power-hungry thug who had killed my mother and left me to die.

"He's going to pay for what he did," I hissed.

Bigsby was unfinished business, business I'd been waiting to resolve for far too many years.

I had thought of nothing but revenge. It'd consumed me, just thinking about the night when the unknown assailant wearing a gold, ruby-and-diamond-encrusted horseshoe ring had shot Mom and me. Mom had died, but I survived.

I'd finally found the owner of the ring—Bigsby. *What are the odds of that?* I had been searching for that ring for years, and it was right under my nose.

But what's Sinthia's connection to Bigsby?

It was something I was determined to find out. It hadn't taken Kevin long to do a thorough investigation, but he hadn't found anything linking Bigsby to her. However, Kevin had dug up some interesting intel about Bigsby looking into Sinthia Michaels's business. If Bigsby was interested in Sinthia, there had to be a sinister motive, which was why I needed to acquire her business fast. Kevin had searched through her background again, looking for anything that could be used as leverage. Surprisingly, Sinthia was squeaky-clean and free of scandal. Frustrated and running out of time and options, I had found a chink in her armor—money.

She required money, and I had lots of it.

That was when I'd swooped in with the assistance of her friend Tabitha Thorp, who had helped me get close to Sinthia. Tabitha had convinced Sinthia of the value of getting an investor —specifically, me—to help her expand her business.

I leaned back in my chair, smiling coldly. Now Bigsby would have to deal directly with me.

My jaw tightened as I glanced impatiently at the watch adorning my wrist.

What the hell is taking her so damn long? Sinthia should have arrived fifteen minutes ago.

I'd give her five more minutes before hopping into my car and driving over to her house to lay down my number one ground rule. When I called, she'd drop whatever the fuck she was doing and haul her sexy ass to my designated destination, or there would be hell to pay.

Ram, my business partner and friend, opened my door and stepped into the office. "Security just informed Zuri that Sinthia Michaels is on her way up." He strode in, closing the door behind him.

I sat forward. "She was supposed to be here fifteen minutes ago!" The words rushed from my mouth like an angry roar.

Ram arched one dark eyebrow. "What the fuck is up with you?" Sitting down in a chair, he propped his feet on my desk, much to my chagrin. "You need to relax, Core. If you bark at her like that, you'll send her ass running out of here, fucking up our plans."

"Do I look like I give a shit?" I retorted, eyeing him coolly.

Ram looked at me as if hinting at something. "Yes, you do," he replied so calmly it raised my ire.

My temper flared. "I don't give a shit about her," I snarled.

Ram grinned like the idiot he was. "Yeah, okay."

I pressed on the bridge of my nose and took a deep breath, pissed that I'd been intrigued by her since we'd met last night at my club. I'd spent the last couple of hours semi-aroused, and it was fucking with my head. This morning I'd woken to a raging hard-on with her name on my damn lips.

It was a real fucked-up predicament. I had no business thinking that way about a woman I was using as bait.

Sinthia was an addictive distraction.

Ram cleared his throat loudly. "Kevin showed me a photo of her. Damn, she's smoking hot." He grinned, leaning back in the chair. "Tell you what. I'm more than willing to take her into my office and show her we mean business...kinky business." He waggled his brows suggestively. "I wonder if she's into handcuffs." He pursed his lips. "Shit, I would love to bend her over my desk, cuff her, and frisk that ass like she's under—"

I put my hand over my face, sighing loudly, and Ram stopped.

But when I looked up again, I had a wicked smile on my face. "You're fucking crazy." I laughed. "But you always know how to calm me down."

"That's what friends do," Ram said.

Ram was more than my best friend. He was the brother I'd never had and the only one I trusted other than a small group of trusted employees. Max and Rocco, my enforcers, roughed up my enemies and kept my business associates in line. Kevin handled the financing and accounting for all of my businesses and my private intelligence-gathering efforts. And Zuri, who was my personal assistant and the little sister I'd always wanted. Ram and I had been through hell and back together. Rising quickly in the world of organized crime, we'd built our empire from the bottom. There were times when I'd thought we'd never make it out alive, but we had. We'd decriminalized our business and turned our lives around.

"Okay, so how do you want to handle this meeting? Good cop/bad cop scenario?" Ram asked quietly.

I took a deep breath and let it out. "No, I'm going solo with this meeting."

Ram gaped at me. "What the fuck do you mean, *solo?*"

For the first time in my life, I opened my mouth, and nothing came out.

Ram's eyes widened. "You want to fuck her?" he asked, shaking his head. "I can't believe it."

I grimaced as the knots in my stomach grew. It took me a good minute or two before I finally managed to get my thoughts together. I gritted my teeth. "Sinthia Michaels is all business, and I'm willing to destroy her business in order to take down Bigsby," I retorted.

I needed Sinthia Michaels as bait, and if that meant she might become a casualty in my war against Bigsby, then so be it.

"Uh-huh." Ram's gaze held a hint of amusement. "We've been friends for a long time. I've learned to read you like a book. You want her."

I leaned back. "I don't need the complication." My life was difficult enough, and I didn't need any distractions, especially now that I'd found my mother's killer. Besides, I wasn't relationship material, and I never would be. I'd fuck women and then show them the door.

Ram's lips twitched. "Yeah, well, that's a damn relief." He looked at me pointedly. "I would hate to have you complicate this mission by fucking her."

Damn. Little did Ram know, shit was already complicated between Sinthia and me.

The phone on my desk rang twice, signaling that Sinthia was

waiting to be guided into my office. Excitement raced through my veins as if I were some high schooler waiting for my prom date.

Damn. What the hell is wrong with me?

Annoyed, I glared at him, my patience gone. "Just escort her in."

Shooting to his feet, Ram gave me a mock salute. "Aye-aye, fearless leader. Let me get my game face on, showing Ms. Michaels that I—" He grinned slightly. "I mean *we* mean business."

I snorted before turning my swivel chair around to face the window. I stood up and clasped my hands behind my back, staring at the Manhattan skyline again.

I heard the huge office door open.

Ram greeted Sinthia formally. "Please come in, Ms. Michaels. Mr. McKay is waiting."

"What's going on?" she asked.

There was utter silence.

"I asked you a question, Mr. Steele," she snapped.

Ram heaved a long-suffering sigh. "Ms. Michaels, a word of advice—if I were you, I would play nice with him. He's in a real fucked-up mood today," he said, his voice clipped, before closing the door with a decisive click.

The soft tapping of heels against the Carrera marble floor alerted me to her approach.

"Sinthia Michaels," I said in a low-pitched voice, "have you brought my money?"

There was a slight pause before she responded, "Money? What money?"

I turned from the window and looked straight at her. My mouth went dry. Lust slithered through my body. Sinthia Michaels was sexy as hell, wearing skintight leather leggings that accentuated her voluptuous curves and a body-hugging black T-shirt that dipped in the front to reveal her tempting full cleavage. My hands could probably span her tiny waist.

Sinthia squared her shoulders as if daring me to say something negative about her attire. She wouldn't get any flak from me. I thought she looked smoking hot.

"You're Core McKay?" She took a step forward, her eyes blazing with rage.

My stare was unrelenting. Sinthia was absolutely gorgeous. She wore her hair pulled back into a tight ponytail, emphasizing her high cheekbones, bow-shaped full lips, and tip-tilted nose. I felt a strange stab of longing deep inside, a strong magnetic pull I hadn't felt about anyone since Maya's death. That loss had devastated me both mentally and emotionally, and it was the reason I'd stayed single and kept my relationships brief with no strings attached.

"Good to see you again, Ms. Michaels." My deep, booming voice resonated throughout the office. "Have a seat. We have a lot to discuss." I pointed to the chair nestled in front of my desk.

She bit her lip as my eyes traveled from the top of her head down her curvy body. Sinthia hesitated, her gaze locking with mine. For a moment, I believed she'd stand her ground, but in an abrupt movement, she conceded, taking a seat.

"Fine." She lifted her shoulders in a shrug. "Listen, I'm going to cut to the fucking chase," she said. "Why the fuck am I here?"

I regarded her for a long time and then sat in the chair behind my mammoth desk. Sinthia shifted, and her jasmine scent wafted into my nostrils, making me want to bury my face against her neck. My cock stirred and stiffened against my pants.

Shit. I had to get over my undeniable attraction to her—and fast.

I smoothed the sleeves of my tailored shirt before running a hand through my hair. "Unfortunately, some disturbing information has recently come to my attention, and it makes me question your ability to make me a profit." My words were civil, but my eyes were hard as granite, letting her know right away that I was in charge.

In a gesture of defiance, she raised her chin and met my eyes.

"No offense, Mr. McKay, but my business deal is with MK Partners." Fire flashed from the depths of her hazel eyes.

If looks could kill, I was sure I'd be dead.

I smirked. Just like I'd thought, Sinthia was a fighter, but she was sadly mistaken if she thought she'd win against me. No one did.

Her eyes widened, her mouth forming a perfect O, when the reality of the situation dawned on her.

"Yes, Ms. Michaels, MK Partners is my investment company," I drawled.

She shook her head. "While that might be true, our agreement was not a loan. I would never take a loan from a man like you."

What the fuck? A man like me?

My jaw tightened. "In your desperation to finance your business, you obviously lowered your fucking highbrow standards," I ground out. I was disappointed she'd been so judgmental without even digging deeply into the kind of man I really was. "Now, the only thing I don't own is your company name. Other than that, I own ninety-seven percent of your precious company."

Sinthia went completely still, her eyes locking with mine. "Impossible," she denied, giving me a suspicious look.

I gestured to the neatly stacked paperwork on my desk. "The impossible became possible, Ms. Michaels." I crossed my arms as I waited patiently for her to comprehend that I had her exactly where I wanted her—under my thumb.

She squared her shoulders before snatching the stack off the desk. Folding my hands in front of me, I projected an air of nonchalance I didn't feel as she slowly scanned the paperwork.

A thrill of excitement raced through my body. Sinthia Michaels was all mine.

Come on, darling. Get with the program and recognize the game is over. Checkmate.

She raised her chin once again. "This is a huge mistake. This wasn't supposed to be a loan. It was a deal for seven percent of my future earnings." She shook her head.

I knitted my brows. "Sinthia"—I tested her name on my tongue—"is that your signature?"

Her mouth tightened. "I swear, this is not what I thought I was agreeing to."

I inclined my head slightly. "Let this be a lesson. Read things thoroughly before you sign." I looked at her coldly. Her mistake was my gain. "Can you pay back my two million dollars plus interest today?"

Kevin had given me a detailed report on her finances. She was living within her means while digging herself out of debt. There was no chance in hell she could raise the money to pay me back.

She sputtered, "What the fuck do you want, McKay? Because —" She stopped mid-sentence as I stared at her with hooded eyes.

She swallowed hard while I allowed my gaze to rake quite intimately over her. Our eyes locked. My groin stirred.

Damn, I love her sexy toughness. It made me want to fuck her senseless.

"You don't expect me to fuck you so you'll forget about this whole loan thing, do you?" Sinthia asked, watching me with disgust.

My lips tilted into a brief small smile. As much as I'd enjoy finding out if she was a hellcat in bed, that wasn't on the agenda —today.

"Do you really think I have to pay to get fucked?" I replied.

She ground her teeth. "Then what do you want?"

Sinthia was trying to bait me, but I wouldn't let her.

"Not a damn thing but my money plus interest," I countered. "I'm not sure you'll be able to produce a profit, darling. My sources tell me your retailers are getting cold feet about the viability of your collection, and they're pulling out of your deals."

She flinched as if I'd physically slapped her. "Bullshit! I have concrete agreements with each of them."

"You really don't know shit about contracts. Nothing in business is concrete. That's what loopholes and a shitload of well-paid lawyers are for." I shot her an irritated glare. "I can tell you don't believe the shit I'm saying, so call Lily Sanchez." I pushed away from my desk and stood up.

"How do you know Lily?" she asked, disbelief ringing in her voice.

I bit back a snort.

Lily was a pawn to maneuver any way I wanted, and she was insignificant in the food chain of New York City power. Lily had been blindsided when her bosses abruptly decided to pull out of Sinthia's deal. Just one phone call to my shadowy connections—who were wealthy, deadly, and ruthless—had killed the agreement.

I'd built alliances while doing things like blackmail, coercion, and extortion, and that had made me one of the wealthiest and most feared men in New York City. Billionaires would quake in their custom-made shoes in fear of being exposed by the cache of intelligence I had about their shady business dealings and sordid sexual tastes. That information would ruin them if I chose to reveal it. I was the puppet master pulling the strings and making CEOs, politicians, and the very affluent dance for my amusement.

I shrugged. "Just call her." I cocked my head. "She'll confirm the gravity of your situation."

She pulled out her cell. Her fingers trembled as she dialed Lily. "Lily, is everything good to go with my collection deal?" Sinthia asked. There was a slight pause before she jumped up, turning her back on me. "What the hell happened?" she whispered. Her shoulders slumped. "I'm two million dollars in, Lily. My collection is almost complete. That's months of work. Do you understand me? Set up a meeting with the financial planners," she snapped before ending the call.

She turned around with her chin lifted. "How do you know Tabitha?"

Raising a brow, I met her angry gaze.

Her eyes widened. "Oh, I see. You're one of her many fuck buddies." Her voice was tight with accusation.

Interesting. Was that a tinge of jealousy I detected in her voice?

"Let's cut to the chase, shall we? I've known Tabitha for years...in various capacities. She knew I was in the market for another lucrative investment, and that's why she came to me when you had financing issues." I pulled out a cigar and a long wooden match. "I had you and your company extensively investigated and found you are very talented." Placing the cigar between my lips, I struck the match and then held it at the end of the cigar. "But, obviously, you're naïve when it comes to business." A surge of flame shot out from the tip of the cigar, and a puff of smoke came from my mouth.

"So do you know where she is?" she rasped.

My lips twitched into a mockery of a smile. "Don't know, and I don't care. But when you find her, give her my regards." I paused, looking at her coolly. "Sinthia, you're tougher than I thought. I like that." I blew a ring of smoke before placing the cigar in the ashtray. "I've come to a decision."

"What decision?" she barked. "You already made a decision when you gave me two million dollars. Now you're making another decision?" She sneered.

So I've hit a nerve. Interesting. I stared, wondering how many more buttons I could push.

"I will make it really simple for you." I crossed my arms and widened my stance. "I've invested two million into your business, and I intend on getting it back plus a hefty profit, so I will retain full control of your company."

She stared at me in astonishment. "This is bullshit! This is my business!" she shouted.

"You mean it *was* your business, Sinthia. Now, it's mine," I replied. "Kevin, my accountant, will take care of all the financial matters, including providing the money to continue your line. In addition, I will make some calls to my contacts to see if we can get your retailers back on board."

My eyes fell to her full lips as she licked them. *Damn, they are absolutely sinful.* My mind roamed to the vision of my manhood sinking deep into her pouty mouth. *Fuck.*

"And all of this is coming at what price?" Her back stiffened. "I will not use my company as a front for illegal business dealings."

I blinked, and then my expression hardened. *Is she out of her damn mind?*

My eyes narrowed. "What the fuck are you talking about?"

She closed her eyes tightly as if she wanted to block the sight of me from her presence. "I've worked too fucking hard to have my business and name tied to anything illegal." She opened her eyes to look at me again.

I stalked over to her, letting my gaze blatantly roam over her sensual body. "What a beautiful hypocrite. There was no thought about where the money was coming from when you took it." I let out a snort of contempt. "Now, you're looking at me like I'm the fucking scum of the earth."

I regarded her silently.

"I'm just calling it like I see it, Mr. McKay. I will not use my business for shady activities." She spat out the words.

I met her frown with a cool look. "Many years ago, I might have used you for that and more. But now, I'm a legitimate busi-nessman." *With dark and twisted connections.*

"What else do you want, McKay?" she asked before licking her bottom lip.

My eyes traveled from her face to her body and then back again. "Oh, darling, I can't begin to tell you all the things I want from you. That would send your gorgeous ass running from this room. But the question is, what do you want, Ms. Michaels?"

"I want you to let me out of this fucking deal," she bellowed.

I laughed without humor. "Not going to happen. Next." I all but sneered.

"If you wanted to, you could," she responded sullenly.

"I'm in the business of making money, not losing it. The deal remains."

Lifting her chin and holding my stare for several minutes, she didn't say anything as I continued to watch her.

She folded her arms across her chest. "This is fucking ridiculous," she roared. "It might be unlawful too."

"Even you don't really believe that shit," I responded with a hard voice.

"And how long is this business arrangement going to last?"

"Until I determine the debt has been paid in full," I bit out, letting my words sink in for a few seconds.

"Fuck you! You might own the company, but you don't own me." She curled her lip in scorn.

The challenge in her eyes filled me with a need I'd never even known I possessed. My hands tightened and unclenched before I caught her by the arm and pressed her against the wall. In one swift move, I pressed my lips against hers. Moving my mouth on hers, I forced her lips open and I plundered inside, one hand tightening on her waist and drawing her even closer. My tongue swept into her mouth while my other hand released her arm, reaching up to wrap itself in her hair, tilting her head back.

Her hands fisting my shirt, she leaned up into me. My mouth devoured and stroked her with a controlled sensuality that made my cock jump to life, straining against my pants to break free. I growled when her mouth widened, and she pushed her tongue into my mouth. I groaned, tasting a hint of mint and coffee.

My head spun out of control as she kissed me back with unleashed anger and passion. The ache within my throbbing balls grew. I knew I wouldn't last much longer until I needed to bury myself inside her cunt.

Sinthia's breath caught as my hands went around her, pulling her away from the wall and flush against me. My fingers traced over her buttocks. She tried to remain motionless, her ass cheeks tensing in reaction. Blood raced to my cock, stiffening it to near pain as I imagined her tight, voluptuous ass clamping down on my cock as I fucked her from behind.

Damn, I burn to have her.

Lifting my head, I broke off the kiss abruptly and stared down at her with hard eyes. "I might not own you now, but I will," I responded with a steely voice before stepping back from her.

Sinthia lowered her head, but not before she seared me with a furious glare. A perverse need for her to acknowledge I was in control overtook me. With slow deliberation, I turned around and strode over to my wall of floor-to-ceiling windows.

"Now you may go, Ms. Michaels." I kept my voice low and soft but left no room for doubt that I'd issued a command.

For several minutes, I waited until I heard the tap-tap of her heels and the soft click of the door closing before I relaxed.

Now that I knew what it could be like between us, one taste wasn't enough. I had to have her. The thought of making her whimper and beg while I took her from behind aroused me more than I would have believed, filling me with the kind of anticipation I'd thought was long behind me.

I wanted her, and that put a completely new spin on everything. My cock jumped as I imagined the possibilities and the challenges of making this work. I needed to banish my ridiculous fixation on her.

Folding my arms, I mumbled aloud, "This shit is about to get really complicated."

❧ 2 ❧

CORE

DAYS LATER

I PULLED UP IN MY LOW-SLUNG PORSCHE AND STEPPED OUT. "I fucking hate Newark," I mumbled, looking around the dirty warehouse.

Ram hopped out of the passenger side, and before slamming the door, he said, "Who doesn't?"

We both headed to the warehouse, slipping into the dark building. Our motorcycle boots sounded like trumpets as they slapped against the hard-concrete floors in the dark, cavernous space.

Rats almost the size of kittens ran across the floor to hide. The air was stale and cloying. Total silence reigned as Ram and I made our way down the metal stairs and through the corridor. Tense and focused, we recognized the importance of this moment. We were one step closer to bringing Lexis, Ram's baby sister, home.

"We're going to find her," I stated through gritted teeth.

"She's been missing for almost a year," Ram grumbled with bleak eyes.

Ram had been blaming himself for her disappearance, for not stepping in when Lexis had gushed about the perfect guy she'd met at a party near her college campus. The guy, Jeff Barolo, had become Lexis's boyfriend after dating her for only two weeks.

Ram had grown suspicious when Lexis refused to introduce Jeff to him, so Ram had driven to her Ivy League school in Massachusetts, only to find out from her friends that Lexis had dropped out of college and run away with Jeff. After a background check, we'd found out Jeff was some preppy wannabe pimp who had a track record for luring pretty college freshmen girls into a life of human trafficking, selling their bodies for sex. It had been hell trying to find any information on the whereabouts of Lexis, because the human trafficking world was dirty and secretive.

One tip after another had led us to dead ends. Every time we'd gotten close to finding Lexis, Jeff would transport her from state to state, changing their location and leaving no trace.

The last hot lead we'd gotten was that she'd been traded between traffickers across the country. After months of attempting to infiltrate the seedy traffickers' world, playing cat-and-mouse games while trying to find her, we'd finally gotten a solid clue from one of the girls with whom Lexis had worked who had escaped Jeff's clutches. She had given us one name. The name, a flashback from our criminal past, was Ben Vargos.

"Where did they find him?" I snapped.

"He's set up shop in the Bronx with some butcher shop as a front." Ram gritted his teeth.

We stood before the door in deadly hunt mode with adrenaline coursing through our veins. This was a slippery slope for ruthless men like us. It had taken us years to leave our criminal lives behind, ones filled with the constant chaos of brutality, most of it perpetrated by us. Now, we were right back where we had started—a life of violence.

Ram grabbed the doorknob.

I clamped my hand on his shoulder. "Let me do this, Ram.

You're in a real fucked-up mood right now. You might end up killing him before we even get any information."

His body stiffened as he turned to look at me. Our eyes locked in battle.

"Core, I can do this without fucking it up."

"You can't, not like this." I narrowed my eyes. "Trust me."

Ram blew out roughly before nodding.

Grinding my teeth together, I stepped into the damp-smelling cell. My eyes quickly adjusted to the darkness as we strode in. Ram closed the door with a decisive click. I nodded curtly to Max and Rocco before my eyes locked on the man in his mid-thirties who was bound to the metal chair sitting between them.

Ben Vargos was unshaven, and his clothes looked slept in.

I sighed heavily. What I was about to do would drag me right back into the criminal world I'd left behind. But we had to get Lexis back, and there was nothing I wasn't willing to do to accomplish that.

Ben's eyes widened. "McKay?" he squawked. His eyes turned to look at Ram. "Ram?"

My nostrils flared slightly before I responded, "Hello, Ben."

Ben glanced around furtively.

The room was silent, except for the low whir of the air conditioner. Ram moved toward the table smack dab in the middle of the room. He snatched up a pair of black latex gloves and impatiently snapped them on.

Ben bucked against the rope binding him to the chair. "Untie me!"

Max growled, slapping Ben on the back of his head. "I will snap your damn neck. Shut the fuck up." Max's voice was flat.

Ben's face contorted with pain. "Core? What the fuck is this shit about?" he squeaked while watching me move unhurriedly toward the narrow table. "I haven't seen your ass in years, and you send your men into my business to drag me out like some punk." He struggled uselessly against the rope.

I ignored him while taking off my leather jacket, folding it, and then laying it over the table ever so carefully. Cracking my knuckles before slipping on my own pair of black latex gloves, I stared blankly at Ben.

His eyes darted toward Ram. "Ram? Come on. We go way back. Talk to Core." Beads of sweat dripped down his forehead.

Ram sneered but remained eerily silent as he moved to sit on the edge of the table.

"Come on, man. This is totally fucked up!" Ben yelled.

I fixed him with a cold stare. "He's not going to save your ass, Ben."

"This is bullshit!" Ben's panic was distinct.

I smiled unemotionally as I rolled up my sleeves, displaying my tattooed forearms. "This is how it's going down. I'm going to ask you some questions, and I want straight answers."

"Fuck you, McKay!" Ben screamed.

I nodded toward the tub of water. Rocco shoved Ben forward, ruthlessly slamming his head under the surface of the water. Ben struggled, but Rocco didn't relent. Ben struggled more frantically until Rocco whipped his head up. Ben gasped for air.

I twirled a chair around, and I sat in front of him. "This is about unfinished business." My eyes were cold, my voice flat. "I hear you've moved up in the world, Ben." I leaned forward. "No more selling underage girls on the corner. You've upgraded to sex trafficking."

Ben licked his lips nervously. "What? No." He shook his head in denial, but the truth was written on his face. "Don't know what you're talking about, man."

Ram's body tensed. "You don't know what he's talking about? You piece of shit!"

He stalked toward Ben before hitting him hard across the face. I watched with disinterest.

"You pimp out underage girls, and when you're done with

them, you sell them to other traffickers," Ram accused as he studied Ben with murderous eyes.

Ben grunted in pain. "Not everyone can go straight like you two."

"I'm going to cut to the chase, Ben." My face remained emotionless. "I know you're part of a sex-trafficking ring that's making a lot of money pimping out college women. I'm looking for one of your buddies, Jeff Barolo."

Ben squirmed. "I don't know him."

I arched a brow. "Our informant says you do. We need to have a little talk with Barolo. And given your precarious predicament, I think you need to be quick about snitching on his whereabouts."

Ben's face tightened. "I'm not saying shit."

Ram shouted, seething with anger, "Where is he?"

I had to move quickly before Ram completely lost it. I bolted to my feet, upending my chair, before shoving Ben forward and bending him over the tub of water. I was done playing around with him.

My voice dropped to a lethal, low whisper. "You either give me the info I want, or I'm going to torture your ass with no mercy."

Ben's whole body trembled. "If I tell you, they'll kill me."

"And if you don't tell me, I'll kill you. So it sounds like you're in a real fucked-up position. But the difference between them and me is I'll make sure you stay alive for five long, agonizing days until you bleed out completely." I smiled cruelly. "Your choice."

"Fuck you, McKay," he spat.

His bravado amused me. "No. Fuck you."

I plunged Ben's head back into the water. He struggled, but not as much as before. I pulled his head back out, and Ben gasped, but I gave him no time before I pushed him back under. Again and again, I forced Ben down. The water stilled. Ben was under, but he'd stopped struggling. When I pulled him out, he didn't gasp for air. His head lolled back, and he was barely coherent. His brow was gashed and raw.

"I know your lungs are burning." I stepped back, drying my hand on a black towel. "I can see the panic in your eyes. You want this to end, and I promise, I will end it. Just tell me what I want to know. Where's Jeff?"

"I don't know." Ben coughed. "Jeff was recruiting women for me, and then I would bring them to my loaded connection to pimp them out to his rolling-in-it friends." He shrugged. "But Jeff got smart. He cut me out of the deal and went straight to my contact, Bigsby Calhoune. He's Bigsby's errand boy now."

"Holy shit," Max mumbled.

My mouth tightened. "Bigsby Calhoune? The politician running for New York City mayor?"

"Yes," Ben responded.

"Bullshit!" Ram barked.

Ben jumped apprehensively. "I'm telling you the truth." His Adam's apple bobbed. "Think about it. Why can't you find Barolo?" He looked around with uneasy eyes. "He's protected by Bigsby. There's a huge demand from his rich friends who think nothing about paying to fuck fresh, untrained women any way and anywhere they want."

Ram snarled, "You fucking bastard."

I grabbed Ram's hand, stopping him from killing Ben. "Go on."

"Jeff fucking me over like he did should have earned him a dirt nap, but I'm not about to make waves with Bigsby since he's helping us clean lots of dough."

Ram's fists tightened at his sides. "Who the hell is *us?*"

Ben gulped. "A bunch of us traffickers got smart. For a huge fee, Bigsby arranged to help us clean our money through his shell company called Pomtonic International. On top of that fee, we're also pumping a hell of a lot of money into UF-Star."

My mind spun with this new information. UF-Star was a super PAC. The independent political action committee had been spending a ton of money to advocate for Bigsby as New York City's new mayor.

I couldn't believe it. After all these years, fate had finally thrown me a bone. I was one step closer to bringing down the man who'd killed my mother. I'd be avenging her death *and* helping Ram get Lexis back in one fell swoop.

"Why the hell are you contributing to UF-Star?" I hissed.

Ben tried to bite back a response. Rocco grabbed the back of his neck and squeezed.

"Once Bigsby gets elected, he'll turn a blind eye to all our illegal activities for a percentage of our profits. That's all I know. I swear." Ben's eyes pleaded. "Look, I told you what you wanted to know. Now let me go."

I leaned forward menacingly while pulling off my gloves before putting them into a black garbage bag. "You actually think I would let a piece of shit like you back on the street?"

Ram smiled coldly before nodding over to Rocco.

Rocco slammed Ben's head into the water. Eventually, the water stilled. He was under, but he'd stopped struggling. When he was pulled up, he didn't gasp for air. His eyes rolled back into his head, and he dropped to the floor. He didn't move.

Ram pulled off his gloves while looking over at Max and Rocco. "Bury him somewhere he won't be found and then clean this place and get rid of all the evidence."

They both nodded.

I pulled out my cell, quickly swiping my finger across it. "Kevin, pull up everything you can on UF-Star and Pomtonic International."

"Will do," Kevin responded before disconnecting.

"I have a feeling once Bigsby finds out we're digging into UF-Star and Pomtonic International, he'll be more than happy to shove Jeff out of hiding and put him right on our doorstep." I looked over at Ram while grabbing my jacket. "Let's go. We have lots of work to do."

ﻬ 3 ﻬ

SINTHIA

I SNAPPED my eyes open to the sound of my cell phone ringing. Grumbling, I rolled over to grab it off the nightstand. "Yes?" I answered.

"Sinthia Michaels?" the man drawled.

Groaning, I sat up in bed gingerly, putting my cell on speaker. "Yes?"

"My name is Kevin Rawley. I've been calling you for days." Kevin's voice sounded annoyed.

I swung my legs over the bed and leaned forward, putting my elbows on my knees and clutching my head. I was exhausted from working on my collection late into the night.

"I left you several voice messages and sent multiple emails."

I could hear the exasperation in his voice.

"And?" I snapped.

"I work for Core McKay. I'm his accountant, and by virtue of your contract with him, I'm now yours too."

Sighing, I sat up before scrubbing my hands over my face. "How can I help you, Kevin?" I stood and decided to get a cup of coffee before taking a nice cold shower.

"Why the fuck do I deal with this shit?" he muttered under his breath. "Like I said on all the messages I left for you, I need access to your business records—more specifically, your invoices."

"No," I responded bluntly while putting on my handpainted silk kimono robe before going downstairs. "If McKay wants my records, tell him to man up, call me, and demand them," I countered.

I stepped into my gourmet kitchen, pressed the button on the espresso machine, and placed a cup beneath the brew head to capture the wonderful stream of black liquid gold.

I was chilled to the bone at the thought of how many things had gone wrong in the last couple months. I had gone from being the sole proprietor of a thriving fashion business—one that had been ready to go live in a matter of months with my highly anticipated Sin Michaels women's wear collection in luxury goods department stores—to none of the retailers willing to return my calls.

Moreover, the most frustrating part of it all was Core McKay, the gorgeous but major asshole, now owned ninety-seven percent of my business. Either I had some pretty fucked-up karma, or fate was just playing a bad joke on me. Either way, I was royally screwed.

"You know what you're doing doesn't make sense," Kevin stated flatly.

"I'm still the designer, and he won't make a damn dime if I decide to sit on my ass and do nothing." When sufficient coffee had flowed into the cup, I lifted it to my lips and took a small sip, savoring the much-needed awakening.

It wasn't about playing games. It was about respect. I wasn't going to stand for McKay sending his minions every time he wanted something from me. And I didn't give a shit that he now owned ninety-seven percent of my business. I wasn't about to bend down and grab my fucking ankles every time the king of bullshit bellowed from his damn iron throne.

"Ms. Michaels, he's going to get what he wants. Fuck it. Let's be blunt. He already has what he wants—ninety-seven percent of your business."

"A valid point. However, I won't be treated like a prison yard bitch."

When he chuckled, I jumped.

"I love your spirit. I truly do, but I'm sure you can't be happy that all your retailers have pulled out of the deal to distribute your collection."

Heat flushed through my body. "No, I'm not."

"And your bills? How are they being paid?" Kevin asked acerbically.

I put down my cup and crossed my arms, staring at my unfinished Sin Michaels collection, which was hanging on racks in parts of my four-thousand-square-foot townhouse.

I sighed heavily.

There was no working around the missing custom fabric I'd ordered. I had no hope in hell of getting it until I paid the overdue bill, which should have been cleared days ago.

"They're not," I muttered.

I didn't feel good about dodging calls from Nia, the president of the fabric distribution company. Moving around some of my assets to make the payment would get the bill paid, but it would also leave me living off next to nothing until my collection hit the high-end retail stores. In theory, that would have worked if they hadn't all pulled out of their agreements to carry my line.

"Play this smart, Ms. Michaels. I've seen the newspaper article that touted you as the next big fashion maven. Don't let your pride dictate your future."

With an aggrieved sigh, I pulled out my notepad. "What's your email address?"

He reeled off his address. I jotted it down before saying, "Check your email in five minutes. I'll send you a link giving you access to all my online business documents and then a separate email with the password." I paused. "Look, I have a massive five-figure bill for custom fabric I ordered. I'm in a real jam, and I can't finish my collection without it. If you could just handle that first, it would be helpful."

"All payments have to be approved by Mr. McKay, so I'd advise you to give him a call," Kevin stated.

"Why can't you just deal with it?" I countered in a sharp tone.

"Because I'm just the accountant. He's the boss. So you need to call him."

"I'll think about it."

"No thinking. Just do it. Let me give you his number," he grumbled.

I rolled my eyes heavenward.

"Sinthia, I'm trying to help."

"Go."

Kevin gave me McKay's number, and I took it down.

"And, Sinthia, stop fucking around. Just call him." Abruptly, he ended our call.

"It was nice talking to you too, Kevin," I replied sarcastically, slamming my cell onto the counter.

4

SINTHIA

Hours later, after sketching until my fingers hurt, I'd had enough of being cooped up in the house. I had a couple of hours to burn before heading over to my scheduled appointment at my friend Francisco "Cisco" Rodriguez's upscale boutique. It was just enough time to partake in some much-needed window-shopping.

Stuffing my cell into my pocket, I grabbed my handbag and stepped out of my townhouse, sighing as the fresh air caressed my face. I loved this time of year. It was right after Labor Day, but the air was still sultry with summer temperatures refusing to go away quietly to make room for fall.

Glancing around my tree-lined neighborhood only a few steps from Central Park, I ran down the stairs before skidding to a stop in the middle of the sidewalk. I shivered from the eerie feeling of being watched.

The more I tried to ignore the feeling, the more creeped out I became. I was paranoid, my eyes darting around as I expected to see my stalker, Jaxon, emerging from the shadows. But there was nothing, only harried New Yorkers hurrying home after work.

"I'm totally losing it," I mumbled.

Deciding to walk instead of taking a cab, I quickened my steps, pushing my way through the Manhattan foot traffic. I loved the energy of New York City. I could meander for hours, but today, I had things to do.

Grabbing a cup of coffee from the coffee cart, I sipped on it while strolling through the heavy pedestrian gridlock. Finally, I arrived at one of my favorite upscale department stores.

I was giddy when I stepped through the double brass doors that kept out the hustle of Manhattan, leaving customers to shop in peace. Like a kid in a candy store, I practically skipped past the chic cosmetic counters. Some people would go to yoga class to relax. My vices were grandiose department stores. I loved to stroll through them, imagining the day my collection would be prettily featured for women to drool over and buy. Even though I had clients to see today, I needed this—just a little me time to dream.

My heart raced with excitement as I wandered through the store, stopping occasionally to touch a garment that caught my eye, before heading to my destination—couture heaven. Riding up the escalator, I arrived at my goal, the prime high-traffic spot on the floor where another trendy designer's clothing line was presented like delicious eye candy.

"Someday," I whispered.

I was so close yet so far. My collection was almost finished, but with my horrible luck, I would be standing at the door, looking in with no entry allowed. The only person who had the power to give me access was Core McKay. One little call—that was what he wanted. Then my business could resume. He would give me the rest of the money. It was stupid and illogical not to swallow my pride and call him, but I knew the call would be a first step down a slippery slope.

Core McKay had thrown down the gauntlet. He was in control, and he wanted me to submit. Just the thought of rolling over in obedience left a bad taste in my mouth.

I was jolted out of my thoughts by the cold drawl of a woman saying, "Still dreaming, huh?"

I recognized the voice. My body tightened. It had been years since I'd heard her hateful, icy tone.

Pivoting on my heels, I turned around to see the one woman I'd never wanted to see again—my narcissistic, alcoholic mother.

"Hello, Grace."

As usual, not one strand of Grace's blond hair was out of place in her tight bun. Her hourglass figure—large chest, small waist, slender thighs—was encased in skintight designer jeans and an expensive-looking silk blouse that showed way too much cleavage. In essence, she looked like a woman desperately trying to look young. It was an epic fail.

"Sin," Grace bit out, wobbling forward.

I scrunched up my nose when I smelled the alcohol seeping from her pores. Grace was drunk, which was nothing new. I'd spent my entire childhood suffering under her drunken tirades and mood swings.

The woman who had given birth to me was still beautiful on the outside. But from the derisive twisted sneer of her lips as she looked me up and down with distaste, she was still a hateful, ugly mess inside.

Grace's frosty blue eyes zeroed in on my body. "I see you're still working on losing those last few stubborn pounds." She smiled. "A personal trainer should fix that right up."

In other words, Grace thought I looked fat.

I smiled coolly. I was far from fat. I was curvy. But from experience, I knew this was Grace's desperate attempt to chip away at my self-esteem to feed her insatiable ego.

That shit is not happening.

When I was a teenager, I'd wilt at her constant digs about my weight. I would run to the bathroom and purge all my food, punishing myself for not being a size six like her. But not anymore. Now, I was a confident woman who'd worked years to heal myself after a lifetime of emotional and mental abuse by

Grace. There was no fucking way she could break me...ever again.

I looked back at her with just as much venom. Then I nodded to the multiple shopping bags she had clutched in her hands. "And I see you're still living a life of champagne dreams on a beer budget," I said disdainfully.

Grace's face hardened.

I smirked. I'd heard through the gossip hags that Grace's teahouse was nearly bankrupt, and she'd been looking for husband number two to keep her in the lifestyle she thought she deserved.

"I'm doing well, you disrespectful wench. Can't say the same for you. After all, you're standing here, lusting after things you obviously can't afford."

I made a face. The woman didn't know shit about me.

"Excuse me, ladies," said a man with a slightly hoarse-sounding deep voice.

I looked up to see him smiling down at me. I stared right back with just as much appreciation. *Dude is hot as hell.* He wasn't too manicured or metrosexual. He was well-groomed with that I'm-not-trying-too-hard look.

Jesus. Yes, please.

"Hello," he said.

He was staring at me, but it was Grace who purred, "Hello." Immediately standing straight while dropping her bags, she ran her pale fingers over her blond hair.

His eyes skated across her with disinterest before returning to rest on me with warmth. A nasty frown crossed Grace's face. For the first time in my life, I noticed the jealous gleam in her eyes. She was looking at me all *Silence of the Lambs*-like, as if she wanted to rip off my skin and wear it like some fucking fur coat.

He smiled wider. "Sinthia Michaels?"

I turned to face him. "Yes?" I answered.

He stuck out his hand. "I'm Nathaniel Butler, merchandising manager for women's clothing. Lily Sanchez reports to me."

I remembered Lily—the energetic buyer from this Fifth Avenue luxury goods department store—had gushed about her hot boss. Well, now I could see why.

I shook his hand before saying, "Nice to meet you, Nathaniel. How's Lily?"

I was distracted when Nathaniel turned our handshake into a half-handshake and half-caress thing before I had the wits to pull my hand away. Disgust was clear on Grace's face as she absorbed our exchange.

He shook his head. "Hell to work with since your deal fell through."

I smiled, knowing Lily's headstrong personality. She'd probably staged a one-woman protest. After all, she was the one who'd pushed for my deal from day one. When Lily had walked into Cisco's boutique and fallen instantly in love with my couture clothing he sold in his store, she'd changed my life forever. In the blink of an eye, at twenty-six years old, I'd moved from fledgling darling of the fashion world to having several luxury goods buyers clamoring to carry my edgy Sin Michaels women's wear line in their stores. But when the stores mysteriously backed away from my deal, Lily had been just as pissed and puzzled as I was.

"At least I have one person who still believes in my collection," I responded.

He smiled. "Two. I wouldn't have backed her idea of bringing your collection to our store if I didn't believe in you." He touched my shoulder. "But all of that is water under the bridge now that your deal is back on the table."

My mouth fell open then closed. "What?"

Nathaniel replied, "It was unfortunate you missed the great conference call we had this morning, but your new business partner, Core McKay, explained you had a meeting conflict. He smoothed over all of the management's concerns over the viability of carrying your collection in our store, and he assured us your clothing line would be delivered on time. It's a relief to be doing business with you once again, Sinthia."

I balled up my fists by my sides. "I'm confused. There was a conference call about my business and my collection this morning?" I swallowed over the lump in my throat. "And your store has agreed to carry my collection again?" I was excited yet pissed about the new predicament. Why didn't McKay inform me about this meeting?

Nathaniel looked uncomfortable as he cleared his throat. "Yes. We're back on board with carrying your collection." He frowned. "Mr. McKay didn't inform you?"

"No, he didn't." My nostrils flared.

Confusion clouded his gaze before it disappeared. "Wait, I get it. He did say you'd be dealing strictly with the creative end of the business, and he'd be handling all the business decisions."

What in the world is going on?

"Excuse me?" My mouth compressed into a thin line.

"I'm sorry. Maybe I misspoke." He looked at his watch. "Anyway, I'm late for a meeting. It was nice seeing you, Ms. Michaels."

He rushed away, leaving me staring at his back.

Grace leaned in with a spiteful mask. "So...having business problems? I'm hiring a hostess at my teahouse. You could always apply."

Her tone ignited my temper.

"You can't afford me," I delivered from between drawn-together teeth. "However, I heard your teahouse is about to be shut down, so you should worry about your own damn self." I smiled coldly. "I think management is taking applications for clerks upstairs. Run along now and apply."

I flipped my hair and walked away with a smile on my face, swaying my hips even though anger was burning in the pit of my stomach.

How dare McKay just take over my business as if he owned it!

I couldn't even see past the rage to the rational side of what he'd done. He'd smoothed things over with at least one retailer. All I could focus on was he hadn't had the respect to tell me about the conference call and his high-handed move of telling the retailer that he was now the decision-maker. This shit would not do.

I stepped out of the store and ran smack into the middle of a throng of pushy New Yorkers when my cell rang. I dug it out of my pocket and immediately recognized the number.

"Hi, Nia," I greeted while navigating my way to Cisco's boutique.

"Hi, Sin," Nia responded. "I've been trying to reach you for days. It's about the shipment of the custom fabric you ordered."

"I apologize, but things have been hectic lately." I pinched the bridge of my nose. Any delay in shipment of the expensive custom prints I'd ordered from Nia's factory in Asia meant the fabric wouldn't arrive in time, halting my whole collection. "I'll get the money by the end of the week. Look, I—"

Nia cut me off, "Sin, what are you talking about? The bill was just paid by your partner, Core McKay. Since it's such a big order, I just wanted to confirm the delivery date so you'd be available to receive it."

I skidded to a stop. A man bumped into me from behind, and he shot me an annoyed glare while grumbling for me to move the hell out of the way. I shot him the bird before walking over to the edge of the sidewalk near a parking meter.

"What the hell are you talking about, Nia?"

Nia cleared her throat. "I spoke to Mr. McKay personally, and he made the payment on your order."

I paused to calm my wildly racing heart. "Please schedule the delivery for Tuesday. Thank you." I hung up, swearing under my breath.

Staring up at the sky, I knew with every twist of fate, the noose was tightening. Whether I liked it or not, Core McKay was making it a point to let me know he was repairing my business, one major fuck-up at a time.

5

SINTHIA

STEPPING OFF THE ELEVATOR, I scanned the studio that had been designed with a contemporary look in mind. I loved the ambiance of Cisco's boutique. The space was sleek, modern, and very glam. The walls were painted black, which allowed the rich colors of my designs on display to pop against the beautiful darkness. Those dark walls also perfectly contrasted with the plush velvet furniture and natural light.

Pulling my tablet from my leather handbag, I quickly took a couple photos of my pieces before flipping through the photos I'd already saved of the gowns I had designed for my bestie Jade Bellisario, her mother Ariana Bellisario, and my new client Erika Watson to wear to Bigsby Calhoune's fundraising gala scheduled for tomorrow night.

I needed to make sure their gowns were perfect. Tonight was the last of three fittings, and I was hoping to get everything wrapped up in time to put the finishing touches on my own gown.

I sighed. *This is going to be a very long night.*

Distracted by my thoughts, I was startled when I heard a squeal.

Then a lilting voice said, "My favorite person."

I didn't even have time to put away my tablet before the petite dynamo rushed up, wrapping her arms around me.

"Hi, Summer." I hugged her and then stepped back with a wide smile. "How's the family?"

She gave me an impish smile. "Crazy," she replied.

I propped my hands on my hips. "You mean *you're* making them crazy."

She waved her hand dramatically. "Me, them—all the same thing." She chuckled. "I completed the alterations on the gowns, and they're waiting for you upstairs." She swung her handbag onto her shoulder. "I have to go and clean up the chaos and mayhem waiting for me at home. Tony's howling like a big bear, wanting to know when I'm coming home. He tries, but God help him, he lets the babies run circles around him."

I snickered because Summer had Tony wrapped around her finger. It was good to see her content after finally finding Tony. She complained about him, but I knew my friend was joyfully grappling with the tornado her adorable newborn twins had unleashed on her home and her big, burly, but lovable husband. I was happy for her but also a little forlorn. I had a small circle of friends, and the circle was getting smaller and smaller every day. They were either in serious relationships, settling down, or getting married.

"Thank you so much for coming in to put the last-minute touches on the gowns. I couldn't have finished in time without you." I really meant it. I hated to take time away from her babies, but Summer was a top-notch seamstress and the only one I trusted to work on my designs.

"I would do anything for my girl Sinthia." She squeezed my hand while smiling warmly. "I doubt you'll need any additional alterations, but call me if you do." She turned on her heel and rushed out.

"Sin, baby!" Cisco exclaimed, rolling his hands about in emphasis. "I haven't seen you in ages."

As usual, he was crackling with energy. Dressed in black

jeans, a crisp blue shirt, and his signature old Rolex, he barely paused before closing the space between us and yanking me into his arms. I hugged him back without any hesitation.

"I've been crazy busy trying to get my collection finished."

He pulled away and clasped my hands. His eyes swept over me from head to toe. At thirty-six, he still looked boyish, but he had intense dark eyebrows that conveyed his seriousness. "Too busy, I see, by the shadows under your eyes."

I scrunched my nose. Cisco was observant and brutally honest.

"I'm exhausted," I snapped, snatching my hands away.

"Mm-hmm."

I rolled my eyes heavenward. "Okay, I'm in a fucked-up mood," I complained.

"Clearly," he responded dryly. He caressed my cheek. "I'm just worried about my Sin. Don't get fucking snarly about it."

I saw the concern flash across his eyes. Instantly, I felt ashamed. Cisco was worried about me like a mother hen.

I softened a little. "I apologize." Wrapping my arm around his lean waist, I dragged him along with me toward the stairs, which led to the dressing lounge.

He draped one arm around my shoulders. "Apology accepted, Sin baby. So any word on Tabitha's whereabouts?"

"Don't get me started. I'm so fucking pissed off right now."

The fact that Tabitha had disappeared without a trace was still confusing. Her cell number was now disconnected, and her boutique had shut down.

I frowned. "She just up and left everything. Who does that?"

Cisco stopped and scowled. "She's a backstabbing skanky bitch. I can't believe she lied to you like that."

"Me either. It just doesn't make sense."

The whole craziness of Tabitha's deception nagged at me. *Why didn't she tell me my investor was McKay?* I felt sick just thinking about her betrayal. When she'd brought me the contract, she'd seemed entirely too happy that she'd found me the deal I needed to solve all my business problems.

Granted, I'd been desperate for financing to help me manufacture my new clothing line, and no bank would have given me a loan until I could dig myself out of the ton of debt I'd accumulated over the years. Tabitha had been my salvation. She'd used her business connections to find me a secret investor who would be willing to provide financing in exchange for a small percentage of my future profits. I'd been practically giddy when I signed the contract with the secret investor and felt the same again when two million dollars had been deposited into my business account with the promise of another million in six months. I'd quickly spent every last dime, paying outstanding business expenses to keep my company running.

My biggest mistake had been not looking over the fine print of the contract or taking the time to find out who the secret investor was. It was a mistake I was still kicking myself in the ass for to this day. But desperation could make you do some fucked-up things, and desperation had introduced the mysterious and eccentric owner of investment company MK Partners into my life.

"I never trusted her. Never," Cisco snapped.

"Let's be clear. I'm not blaming her for my stupidity in signing the damn contract without looking at the fine print." I pointed to myself. "That fucked-up move is all me. But, damn, I trusted her as my friend. She could have been straight with me and told me Core McKay was the investor. She owed me that much."

Her betrayal had stung the most. Tabitha had been my mentor, and I'd thought she was my friend.

"But to leave her successful business and disappear? That shit is crazy," I said flatly.

His eyebrows shot up. "Successful? Her business was only making money from the pieces of your collection you'd allowed her to sell there."

"She had a little creative dry spell."

"God, how can you still defend that bitch?"

I shot him an annoyed glare. "I'm not defending her. I'm just stating a fact."

"And I told you months ago about the rumors circulating regarding her money problems."

"Tabitha always had money problems. Her income could never support her lifestyle."

Even after a lengthy stint as the go-to designer for several celebrities, Tabitha's extravagant lifestyle and years of partying and jet-setting more than she was designing had taken a toll on her business. But she'd still managed to stay afloat—or so I'd thought.

"Exactly," Cisco responded.

"I don't want to talk about Tabitha." I grabbed his hand and pulled him along, deciding I needed to change the topic fast. "So how's your newest acquisition?"

"Young and hung." He laughed huskily. "Jesus, he does this thing with his tongue and my ass that makes my toes curl." He waggled his eyebrows. "Oh, and did I mention he's also a master at—"

I skidded to a stop, holding up my hand. "Don't you dare say it, Cisco."

His eyes widened with fake innocence. "But—"

I slapped my hand over his mouth. "Don't. I get it. He's gifted. Stop trying to make me jealous."

He started talking, but thankfully, it was muffled by my hand. I removed it.

He smiled in his simply gorgeous way. "Only if you promise to have lunch with me this week. I miss hanging out with you."

I grabbed his face and kissed him soundly on both cheeks. "I will."

"Good. Now hurry your sexy ass upstairs to the lounge. The fitting rooms have been set up. Yell if you need anything."

I stepped away, waving my hand over my shoulder. I hurried

off, dashing up the stairs and into the cream-colored lounge. A champagne bottle was open, glasses waiting. Dropping my bag, I checked each fitting room to see which one had whose gown before pouring myself a flute of champagne. Kicking back, I flipped through my designs on my tablet.

Jade sauntered in, and she flopped down beside me.

"Rough day?" I handed her my glass before pouring another for myself.

She guzzled her champagne like water. "Erika was a real hag today. She made me do a zillion takes just to flex her I'm-the-producer-of-this-damn-show muscle."

"I don't blame her. She's frantic because you're going to be away for months in New Zealand on your movie shoot."

I was very proud that Jade was finally making her dream come true. She was taking the script she'd written and was independently producing a movie.

"So she makes me shoot longer scenes as punishment." She sulked playfully. "I'm not just a pretty face, you know. It's emotionally draining, running the gamut of gut-wrenching scenes."

"Oh, poor baby. Starring in a smoking-hot television series is so much work." I pointed to the dressing room. "Now get your ass in there and change. I have lots of shit to do tonight, actress extraordinaire."

Jade's apple-green eyes narrowed. "Come on. Give me a minute." She plopped her feet onto my lap. "I'm exhausted."

I pushed them off. "The gala is tomorrow night, and this is your last fitting. Go. I can't have you looking like a hot mess in my creation."

Jade stood up and swayed away, mumbling under her breath about my lack of respect for her craft.

"Oh my goodness, Sin," she squealed from inside the dressing room. She peeped out, grinning from ear to ear. "It's beautiful."

I grinned right back and said, "Change, Jade."

The two-piece ensemble was risqué, but as usual, Jade wasn't afraid to let the fashion take the lead, which was one of the many things I loved about her.

"And the designer can't accept compliments," she grumbled before popping her head back in.

Two glasses of champagne later, I yelled, "Jade!" There was total silence. "I know you're dressed and taking selfies. Get your skinny butt out here. Now."

"You're so bossy today."

She sauntered out, looking every bit one of Hollywood's most beautiful actresses as she flaunted her perfect body in my couture design of a midriff-baring white crop top with a flowing skirt. She turned around, examining her ass in the floor-to-ceiling mirror, doing a perfect imitation of a dog chasing its tail.

"Sin! Fix my skirt. It's hanging funny around my ass."

Leaning back against the soft, comfy gray couch, I sipped champagne, watching with amusement. "What do you want me to do about it?"

"You designed it. Fix it." She frowned.

"God, you're such a whiny baby," I huffed before getting up and walking over.

Jade spun around in the mirror. "I'm your bestie, so I'm entitled. Fix it. My ass looks unspectacular."

"That's because it requires more ass." I smiled saucily before twisting the skirt until it lay perfectly.

I stepped back, examining her in the white gown. The two pieces accented her lean body. She was the best walking commercial for my clothing line.

She laughed huskily. "Not everyone is blessed with a sexy ass like you." She grabbed my glass before taking a sip.

I smiled. "What can I tell you? Ass is in, and I'm riding the motherfucking bootylicious wave, baby." I reached in and hugged her. "And thank you for wearing my dress to the gala."

Just the press coverage of Jade, the most desired and in-demand actress right now, would be enough to keep the fashion hags talking for days.

She fanned me away. "Please. You make me look sexy. Besides, if you made a dress out of plastic bags, I would proudly wear that shit." She winked.

That was why I loved her so much. Despite the money and fame, she remained humble and real.

Jade shook her long black hair. "So how did your day go?"

"Sugar and spice," I said. "I spoke to my new accountant today, Kevin...McKay's minion."

She fluffed up her hair. "What do you think? Up or down?"

"Up." I walked behind her, twisting her hair up into a high, loose knot. "Like this but less messy."

She preened in the mirror. "Up it is." She shook out her hair, letting it cascade over her shoulders and down her back. "So what was Kevin the accountant like?"

I tightened my mouth. "He seemed like an okay guy. Just a little pushy. He kept going on and on about me calling McKay, and he gave me his number." Stalling, I flicked at the nonexistent dust on her shoulder. "Oh, and I found out McKay paid my outstanding bill for the custom fabric I ordered."

Her mouth dropped open. "That bill was five figures." Her eyes narrowed at my frown. "That's a good thing, right?"

I shrugged. "I guess. I also found out he got one retailer back on board with carrying my collection."

"Okay. So what's with the sour face? You should be jumping up and down with joy—or at the very least, planning a scorching hot lap dance for Mr. McKay."

I shook my head. "You do realize a lap dance isn't exactly the solution to every girl's problems?"

Jade screwed up her mouth. "Says who?"

I groaned. "Moving on because it's just too exhausting to debate about your theory right now."

"Well, it seems to me McKay is doing all the right things by you."

"I beg to differ. He had a conference call with the retailer this morning and didn't bother to invite me."

She jammed her hands on her hips. "Uh-huh. And why does that matter?"

My eyes widened. "Because I'm a part of this business. I'm not just the hired help."

"There could be a plausible reason for his oversight."

I walked toward the settee before sitting down. "Like what?"

She rolled her eyes heavenward. "Like why don't you fucking ask him? This shit is ridiculous. Woman up. Pick up the phone and call him."

"Negative on that idea." I rolled my shoulders to relieve the tension. "Do you think I'm cursed? Because it feels like it."

"Cursed? Blessed is more like it. He paid off your fabric distributor bill and smoothed things over with at least one retailer." Jade blinked her eyes humorously. "Holy shit! Yes. He's a damn monster," she finished mockingly.

"He didn't do it because he's a saint."

She strolled over to the sofa and sat down with a loud sigh. "You're damn right. He did it because, guess what? He's a businessman. Has it even crossed your mind that your approach to your predicament is all wrong?"

I sat straight up. "Oh, hell no! Don't go all Zen bananas on me."

She held up her hand. "Don't get mad. Just listen to me. I know men."

I frowned. "And I don't? I haven't fucked in a while, but that doesn't mean I'm hopelessly out of commission."

"I'm going to ignore that statement because it's just too much work to go into why it's just...well, all wrong." She gave a quick shake of her head. "Jesus. Have you learned nothing from me all these years?"

"Oh, I've learned plenty from your too-much-information recaps of your sexual escapades. Lesson number one"—I counted off on my fingers—"breathe through your nose, not your mouth, when trying to take a cock to the back of your throat without gagging. Number two, a Dirty Sanchez isn't for the fainthearted.

Oh, and the most important lesson"—I batted my eyelashes almost comically—"have lots of painkillers on standby after getting fisted." I smiled saucily. "All good lessons. Thank you."

Jade winked at me. "Well, you know me. I'm willing to do all the hot, sweaty research for the betterment of your fuck game."

"I haven't had any complaints yet."

"Because of me doing all the damn legwork." She slapped my thigh. "But let's not get distracted. Back to McKay."

I reclined. "No. I'm tired of talking about him."

"All I'm saying is you're fighting fire with fire and getting absolutely nowhere with him. Honey is what's needed." She fluttered her eyelashes, tossing her hair dramatically. "Like that. But with you, you've got to spread it on thick and wear something low-cut when you're doing it."

I looked at her like she'd lost her ever-loving mind. "Not going to be able to do it."

"Okay. Your choice, but he's holding all the cards."

I scoffed. "He's a prick." *Gorgeous and smoldering, but undeniably, he's a bona fide asshole.*

"Grasshopper, that shit doesn't matter. All that matters is you're making yourself miserable over a deal you're stuck with until he chooses to end it. Do you know how many deals I've made that suck ass? Too many to fucking count, but I made them because I had to give a little so those Hollywood movie executive pricks would even consider me for prime roles."

"He took ninety-seven percent of my business."

"He's the bank, and you're the creator. You both need each other."

"But—"

Jade interrupted me. "It doesn't matter why this shit happened, but it did. He gave you two million dollars and an accountant. Use this opportunity to learn what makes him tick, and work the man until you can flip this deal and change the business stake on paper."

I groaned painfully. "I know I should, but I can't."

She shook her head. "I love you, but you're driving me crazy with your stubbornness." She arched a brow. "Let's keep it real. You're a talented designer, but keeping the books isn't your forte. You can barely balance your fucking checkbook. I think it makes perfectly good business sense to have someone manage your finances. It's no biggie. If McKay wants to pay all your expenses, let him."

I exhaled loudly. I hated that she'd picked the most inopportune time to be logical.

"Sin, I'm telling you to play nice with him. Now, put on your big-girl panties and then call him and thank him...nicely."

"I can't."

"Why?"

My body tensed. "Because that's exactly what he wants me to do."

"You mean that's what you want to do, and it scares the shit out of you."

Damn it!

I couldn't hide shit from Jade. It'd been that way since the first day we met as freshmen in high school, and it would always be that way.

"Yes, it does." My fascination with McKay was fucking strange and sordid. I'd been masturbating almost every night since my last meeting with him. My vibrator, Beast, simply couldn't handle the pressure. "On a business level, I get him. He's all about money and work. It's the personal side that scares me because I can't read him." *Or trust myself when I'm around him.* "One minute, he looks like he wants to devour me. The next, he looks like he wants to kill me. He's crazy."

"Excuses. It's not complicated, Sin. You're tearing yourself up for nothing." Jade arched a well-manicured brow. "Just swallow—"

I cut her off. "I will not give him a blow job."

"Uh..." She smiled. "I was going to say swallow your pride and call him. But I'm all for you taking the blow-job approach."

I scoffed. "I'll just call him."

Jade was right. I had to call him. Things between McKay and me couldn't go on the way they had been. Maybe I was building this friction thing between us to be a bigger thing than it was.

I jumped up, pulling my cell out of my pocket as I braced myself to make the call I'd been dreading for days.

This madness between McKay and me had to stop.

Her face dropped with disappointment. "Okay. You could do that, but the BJ is much more fun and creative."

My mind raced while I paced. On one hand, I disliked him. On the other, I wanted to fuck him. I was on the verge of snapping like a twig from the stress.

She rolled onto her stomach on the sofa, propping her chin on her hands.

I stormed over to her and slapped her arm. "What are you doing? You're rolling around in a couture evening gown."

She fanned me away. "Stop stalling. And don't forget to put it on speaker. I want to hear it all."

I plopped down next to her, scrolling down my contact list, and touched his number, automatically calling it. I pointed at her, putting it on speakerphone. "I'm going to cunt-punt you down the stairs if you make a sound," I whispered.

She made the zipping motion across her mouth.

"Hello?" he rasped in a gravelly voice.

My heart thumped at the allure of his voice. *Get it together, Sin.*

She whacked my arm and mouthed, *Oh my God!*

I jabbed her in the side and mouthed, *Shut up!*

"It's Sinthia Michaels," I croaked, suddenly feeling like an insecure high school girl. I counted to ten before saying, "I wanted to say thank you for calling the retailer and for paying my distributor."

He took so long to reply I thought the line had disconnected.

"Are you still there?" I asked impatiently.

"I'm only cleaning up the shit you got yourself into."

I straightened my back. "What did you just say?"

"I've reviewed your business records, and I found the steady decrease in your income. I also noticed the few business deals you've made are ridiculously unprofitable."

I wanted to claw his damn eyes out.

He continued, "I will not lose money on this business deal. I'll give you free rein to steer this business creatively, but I'll make all the strategic decisions from this point on."

I jumped up and marched up and down, feeling my frustration mount. "This is my company, and I will not be relegated to some corner while you run *my* business," I hissed. "You might have a major stake in my company, but there is no Sin Michaels collection without me. So this is how it's going to go, McKay. Regardless of what's on that fucking contract, you will treat me as an equal partner."

The phone was silent.

"Hello?" I shouted.

"Ms. Michaels, don't ever give me an ultimatum," he said in a brisk tone. "You might have creative control, but that doesn't mean shit without my fucking money." Without another word, he ended our call.

I gaped at the phone in shock. "He hung up on me." I stared at Jade. "He's an asshole."

She smiled. "I disagree. He's just not putting up with your shit. He's alpha delicious." She moaned like a porn star. "The man is sex on a stick, and he's ready to blow your back out, girl."

I sat down beside her. "You sound like a lunatic. That shit is not happening."

"Yet." She smiled smugly.

"Ever," I snapped.

McKay might have my livelihood in his hands, but now I was determined to find a way out of his clutches—the sooner, the better.

Jade scooted to sit up. "I know that look, Sin. Your mouth

says no, but your mind and body are saying completely the opposite." She waggled her eyebrows.

I gave her the evil eye. "Are you trying to make me shank you?"

Ariana breezed in with her new bestie, Erika Watson, walking beside her.

"Cate, enough!" Ariana screamed into the cell pressed against her ear.

"Hello, Erika," I said.

Erika kissed me on the cheek before dropping her outrageously expensive designer bag onto the sofa like it was a sack of greasy fast food. "All the way over here, they've been at it on the phone." She rolled her eyes. "If I wanted to hear that shit, I could have stayed at work and listened to the overpaid divas bitch about who has more lines."

"Are you talking about Jade?" I winked at her.

I loved Erika. She was remarkably laid-back for a woman who'd achieved so much so fast. She was an award-winning writer and producer who created hit TV shows. She was also the first African-American woman to create and executive produce a top ten network series, a series starring Jade.

Erika smirked. "I refuse to confirm or deny that shit." She looked Jade up and down. "I love you in that gown." Erika grinned at me. "Are you ready for me to get all sexy?" She poured a glass of champagne.

"You're set up in the second room," I responded.

"I'm done with this conversation, Cate," Ariana growled into the phone.

"Thank God." Erika grimaced, eyeing Ariana. "Ariana and Cate are like two pit bulls in skirts." She swayed toward the fitting room before slamming the door behind her.

"Good-bye. Yes, I'm hanging up, Cate," Ariana barked before tossing her cell into her handbag. "I'm going to kill her."

Jade arched a brow. "So what's the self-appointed queen bee of the Bellisario clan bitching about now?"

Jade was the daughter of Ariana Bellisario—a philanthropist, heiress, and successful businesswoman—making Jade a member of the illustrious group of New York socialites. Her aunt, Cate Bellisario, was older than Ariana by a couple years. To some, that made Cate the most powerful member of the Bellisario family. She was using that status among the city's elite to get her fiancé, Bigsby Calhoune, a wealthy shipping mogul, elected as New York City's mayor.

"Anything and everything." Ariana flopped down next to me and smiled. "How are you, darling?"

"Better than you, I gather," I said.

"Mom?" Jade asked.

Ariana sighed. "She's micromanaging the shit out of this fundraising gala." She rolled her eyes heavenward. "Bigsby arranged a family photo opportunity at the gala with a major magazine. *Arrive early*," she mocked Cate's whiny voice.

I laughed because it'd sounded exactly like Cate. New York City's queen socialite bitch Cate had handpicked the rich elite and A-listers for the fundraising gala, and they had been granted the opportunity to get all gussied up in honor of her fiancé. The gala was the biggest event on the high-end social calendar. The ten-thousand-dollars-per-ticket gala was meant to raise funds for Bigsby's mayoral race, but in reality, it was just an excuse for a self-celebratory orgy of red-carpet posing.

"Blah, blah, blah. God, I hate that fucker Bigsby," Ariana hissed.

"Exactly!" Jade chimed in. "He reminds me of some two-bit used car salesman."

I shuddered. "He just gives me the creeps."

He did. He always seemed to be leering at me like some perverted slimeball.

Ariana pointed at me. "Exactly. You hit the nail right on the head. He's creepy. That's why I hired a private investigator. I'll be damned if I let my sister marry that sleazy bastard."

I gave Jade a sidelong stare. "Does Cate know?"

Jade nodded. "Hell yes. We're the last members of the Bellisario dynasty and each worth millions. If you want to date a Bellisario, you get investigated thoroughly. Most guys just bow out ungracefully because they can't deal with Irvin, the investigative proctologist."

I arched a brow. "He's that thorough?"

Ariana pursed her lips while pouring champagne. "Yes, but surprisingly, he didn't find shit on Bigsby."

"That's a good thing, right?" I inquired.

Ariana's eyes narrowed. "No, not when it comes to Bigsby. Irvin is suspicious. He says Bigsby's records were too squeaky-clean. Irvin's still digging. If there's something to find, he will find it. Believe me."

"See, Sin? This is the shit rich people have to resort to. We don't know the meaning of trust because everyone has a side game. At least with McKay, he's keeping it real."

I shot Jade a warning stare. "Shut up."

She shrugged. "Don't shoot the messenger."

"What's going on with you two?" Ariana looked at me and then Jade.

Jade nodded in my direction.

I sipped my champagne, avoiding eye contact with Ariana.

"Sin?" Ariana queried.

I looked at her sheepishly.

She pursed her lips. "Jade?"

Jade looked at me pointedly and whispered loudly, "She wants to have sex with a banging hot billionaire."

I gave her the one-finger salute. "I hate you so much right now."

Jade blew me a kiss.

Ariana swatted at Jade. "Leave her alone."

"Hello? I'm trying to help," Jade responded.

I frowned. "So annoying."

Ariana patted my hand. "I know, sweetie. She can be like that piece of corn you can't quite get out of your teeth. Annoying." Ariana smiled sweetly, too sweetly, at Jade.

"I love you too, Mom," Jade mumbled under her breath.

Ariana eyed me. "Now are you going to tell me who's the lucky man and why you look so pissed off about him?"

"I'm angrier at myself." I had to take responsibility for my actions. I hadn't looked at the fine print on the contract. It was a total idiot move. "Stupidly, I signed a business deal with the devil, giving him my soul and ninety-seven percent control of my business in exchange for financing," I blurted out in one breath.

Ariana sat straight up, spilling her champagne. "Ninety-seven percent? Who's the lucky devil?"

"Core McKay," I responded.

She shot me an incredulous stare. "Billionaire Core McKay?"

"Yep, that's the devil incarnate."

Ariana scowled. "If you needed financing, why didn't you come to Jade or me for the money?"

"Don't blame her, Mom. She couldn't borrow the money from me because my assets were tied up in my indie movie project."

Ariana pursed her lips. "Okay. What about me?"

I sighed heavily. "I love you, but I can't go running to you and Jade every time I have money problems." I grabbed her hand when I saw the flash of sadness in her eyes. "I wanted to do this on my own."

She squeezed my hand back. "You're not on your own. You're like my daughter, and if I can help, I'll do it, no questions asked." She nudged me playfully with her elbow. "But I get it. You want to be independent. There's nothing wrong with that, but be independent *and* smart."

I leaned my head on her shoulder. I loved Ariana because she was beautiful inside and out.

When Dad died and Mom disowned me, Ariana had taken me into her family, treating me like I was her daughter. Yes, I knew Ariana would have loaned me the money, but that was a line I would never cross. Family and business did not mix. I'd learned that the hard way with Grace.

"I had it under control—or at least, I thought I did."

Ariana and Jade scowled at me.

"Okay. Fine. I'm stubborn and irrational. I know this. I'm paying for my flaws right now."

I kissed Ariana's cheek, and that seemed to pacify her.

"Next time I get into a jam, I'll at least call you to get advice before I proceed."

Ariana hugged me. "See? That wasn't so hard." She sat back, settling in like she had nothing but time.

My eyes widened. "Oh no, you don't. Can you please get in there and get dressed?"

She smiled, putting up her hands. "Okay, I'm going." She grabbed her glass. "Which room?"

I pointed to the last dressing room on the left, and she happily swayed off.

Jade slid off the couch and stood on wobbly legs, most likely from way too much champagne. "I've got to get out of here. I have a hair appointment," she said before rushing over to the dressing room.

HOURS LATER, I WAS ELATED TO HAVE SOME PEACE AND QUIET. Jade and Ariana had already left, and Erika was getting dressed. This allowed me to sit on the couch, sipping the last of the last bottle of champagne, while finishing up business.

Erika came out, fully dressed in her street clothes. Smiling at me, she grabbed her bag and handed over a check.

I gave her a questioning look. "This isn't the price we agreed on. You overpaid by three thousand dollars. I can't take it."

She waved away my objection. "It's for all your help and for rearranging your schedule to make my gown for tomorrow night." She looked at me shrewdly. "I hope you don't get offended, but I overheard your conversation with Jade and Ariana about your contract issues."

"I'm not remotely close to giving up designing for a job at a fast-food restaurant."

"I know, but money means nothing to me these days, and if I can help in any way, I will. It sounds like you need help and fast," Erika drawled. "I have an excellent attorney whom I trust implicitly—Mitch Fillion, my husband."

My eyes widened. *How did I not know she was married to him?*

Erika dug into her ridiculously expensive designer bag before passing me a business card. "He's the best damn attorney in New York City, if I do say so myself."

I eyed her. "You're married to Mitch Fillion?"

"Recently married. We're still newlyweds." She waved her fingers, displaying the large, sparkling diamond engagement ring coupled with the diamond-encrusted wedding band. "I'm wife number two." She pursed her lips. "Wait, is it number three?" She laughed huskily. "Shit, it doesn't matter because that man is a genius in the bedroom." She shivered deliciously.

Why do my clients insist on oversharing?

Most people would be surprised at how much personal information my wealthy and famous clients shared with me. From the benign tidbits about who just got cosmetic surgery and butt implants, to steamy shit like who was fucking whose husband, to lovers fucking lovers, to who was caught at the McKay Club in the private kink room, to wives fucking employees, to husbands fucking butlers, and threesomes and foursomes—it was all one big fuckfest in the world of the rich and privileged. None of the gossip I really cared about, but with all the information, I could make a shitload of money by writing a scandalous tell-all book that would cause fucking chaos.

I shook my head and said, "Thanks, but no thanks. There is no way I'm calling him."

Her eyes widened. "Why?"

I swallowed over the pain and embarrassment, which still

stung to this day. "Because his son Kyle is my old high school boyfriend and a prick. Frankly speaking, the apple doesn't fall too far from the tree."

Erika's face tensed. "Kyle really hurt you." She reached out and grabbed my hand.

"It's more how I made a fool out of myself for him."

Her grip tightened. Normally, I wasn't a touchy-feely woman with strangers, but her rich chocolate eyes that reminded me so much of Dad's, combined with the warmth and comfort of her touch, put me surprisingly at ease.

"I know you blame Mitch, but believe me, he had nothing to do with how that arrogant, spoiled prick turned out. That's all Mitch's ex-wife's doing." She sighed. "That woman is a real piece of work. She's fucking nutty." Erika quickly pulled her hand away as if she'd just realized she was still clutching mine. "Please just call Mitch. He's not like you think he is. He's a good man. Plus, like I said, he's the best damn attorney in New York City."

Maybe that was what I needed. A devious, ruthless fuck would be necessary to get me out of the contract with McKay.

I shoved the card into my handbag. "I'll think about it."

"Wise decision. Sometimes, we have to align ourselves with people who will help us get to our ultimate goal, and there's no shame in that." She winked at me before walking away. "See you tomorrow night."

✥ 6 ✥

SINTHIA

I PACED BACK AND FORTH, my mind spinning. I stopped and stared at his business card. *How bad can he be if he's married to a woman like Erika?*

My mind spun around the fact that my life had turned full circle. I was seeking help from the man whose son had destroyed my self-confidence for years. I knew I shouldn't lump all assholes together, but it was hard not to.

I blew out heavily before quickly tapping the phone number shown on the card into my phone.

"Mitch Fillion," he clipped out.

I licked my lips, which had gone desert dry. "Hello, Mr. Fillion. My name is Sinthia Michaels. I was referred to you by Erika."

I was a little relieved when his voice held a softer edge as he said, "How can I help you?"

"I have a business issue. I need help with a contract."

"You need me to look over a contract?"

I wiped my now sweaty palm over the leg of my jeans. "No. I need you to help me break it."

"Who is the contract with?"

I exhaled slowly. "MK Partners."

The silence on the line lasted so long that I thought our call had gotten disconnected.

"Hello?" I asked.

He cleared his throat. "I'm sorry, Ms. Michaels, but Mr. McKay has me on retainer."

I squeezed my eyes shut. *Shit.*

"Well, this is awkward," I mumbled while my mind whirled around one question. *Will Fillion tell McKay I called him about breaking our contract?*

I clenched my fists.

There was no doubt in my mind the answer to that was yes. *Damn! McKay is going to be fucking pissed.*

He didn't seem like a man who would take kindly to the fact that I was trying to outmaneuver him.

"Since my wife referred you to me, she must hold you in high regard, so I can recommend an excellent attorney who might be able to help you."

"Sure. Thank you." I went over to my workstation, grabbed a notepad, and scribbled the name and number he gave me. "Thank you, Mr. Fillion," I said before clicking off.

Jesus. I am so screwed.

DRESSED AND SITTING ON THE ARM OF MY LOVE SEAT, I swirled the red wine in the glass as I stared at the clock. Jade was late again. I was already disgruntled about agreeing to go to this ridiculous gala in honor of the one man, Bigsby Calhoune, whom I did not intend to vote for as mayor. But I'd agreed to be Jade's plus-one, and I didn't renege on promises to friends, no matter how badly I wanted to.

My cell rang. It was a private number. "Hello?" I answered.

No one responded, so I hung up.

The cell rang again with a private number. I said, "Hello?"

Nothing.

"Who the fuck is this?"

Heavy breathing.

"Fuck off, pervert." I swiped my finger across the screen, ending the call.

The doorbell rang. I walked toward the entry. Peering through the peephole, I saw Jade standing on my stairs, looking annoyed but strikingly beautiful. Opening the door, I stared at her features highlighted with smoky eye shadow, a smidge of blush, and a slick touch of rose-pink lip gloss. Her nails, painted a bright shade of red, tapped against the doorframe.

"You're late," I snapped.

She held up her hand. "Don't even start with getting all anal about me being late," she responded while crossing the threshold.

I slammed the door behind her.

Rudely, she snatched my glass of wine out of my hand and took a sip.

"Uh, you take my Jesus juice without so much as a hello?" I asked.

"I'm sorry." She kissed my cheek before guzzling more of the wine. "I swear this gala is going to be the death of me." She swallowed another gulp of wine. "I lost precious brain cells while mediating another argument between my mother and Cate over the fact that Mom and I refuse to take part in the special photo op Bigsby arranged at the gala."

I strolled over to the kitchen, grabbed another glass, and poured wine into it. "Sounds like rich people's drama," I said in a singsong voice.

"Yeah, yeah, I know. People are dying of hunger while my family's number one concern is with whom we will or will not take a photo. Trifling but true." Jade drained her glass and stared at me. "On a lighter note, you look absolutely gorgeous, Sin."

I spun around, showing off the backless part of the sleeveless beaded gown with a revealing plunging neckline that barely hid my belly button. The only thing keeping my full breasts from falling out was the discreet beaded hook right below each. I twerked my ass, calling attention to the back of the gown that was cut low to show off my back tattoos.

I turned around to face her and asked, "So what do you think?"

"First, did you just twerk? I think you've been watching way too many music videos." Jade's lips curled up into a smile. "Second, wow, I love the vintage vibe of your gown. How you've managed to pull off a look that's elegant and includes a little butt crack is beyond me." She tapped her bottom lip. "But you're missing something. Don't you have some vintage jewelry to wear?"

"My diamond cuff bracelet. I could throw that on."

She frowned. "No. Not retro enough. Wait. I got it. Remember that Victorian-looking silver bracelet your father gave you for your birthday? Wear it."

My heart thudded. "Yeah, um…" I licked my lips anxiously. "I don't want to wear it. Way too many sad memories." It was stupid and pathetic, but I'd compartmentalized all my memories of Dad years ago, stowing them in a trunk I'd shoved into my guest bedroom. Out of sight and out of mind was my goal.

She glared at me. "Sin, where did you hide it?"

I swallowed a large mouthful of wine. "Trunk in my spare bedroom." I rolled my eyes. "Don't give me that look. I haven't had many opportunities to wear it." Well, that part was true, but the most important reason was the bracelet caused too many emotions to surface—happy and sad.

She sighed heavily. "You can't continue to blame yourself for his death, Sin. You were young. You argued with him, but you didn't cause that reckless driver to slam into him."

I blinked back the tears and fought the impending guilt. "He was driving around that night, looking for me." The memory of that morning and the shouting match I'd had with Dad still made my heart heavy with emotion.

It was my birthday, and I was so excited Kyle was going to take me out for lunch after school. I bounced into the kitchen, intending to grab a yogurt before heading out, only to stop at the sight of Dad flipping pancakes at the stove.

"Dad? What are you doing here?" I was happy to see him.

Normally, he'd leave for work before I got up in the morning, and he'd come in late at night after I was already in bed.

He turned, grinning at me. "I'm going in late. I couldn't miss making a birthday breakfast for my little girl."

I rolled my eyes heavenward. "Not little. I'm seventeen today," I boasted before eyeing the small box wrapped in pink-and-green paper on the table.

He smiled indulgently. "Yes, it's for you."

Snatching up the box, I ripped off the paper and then pulled off the top. Nestled inside was an agate silver bracelet. "Oh, Dad, I love it." Running over to him, I hugged him. "Thank you so much."

He kissed my forehead. "Give me your wrist."

I could barely stand still from excitement as he clasped the unusual bracelet around my wrist.

He grabbed my face softly. "Sin, this bracelet is very special. It's an heirloom which belonged to my Scottish great-grandmother. It's the only piece of our heritage our family has left." His eyes clouded over with emotion. "Promise me you'll cherish it."

"Always, Dad."

"Good." He nodded before stepping back and picking up a plate stacked with pancakes. "Sit down. The pancakes are getting cold," he ordered before resting the plate on the table.

Plopping down at the kitchen table, I gave him a wobbly smile. Dad looked tired. Dark shadows were under his eyes. His tall frame looked gaunt. I tightened my fists, hating Mom for forcing him to work longer hours so she could live the lifestyle of the elite.

He sat down, and I tucked into my pancakes.

"You're not eating?" I asked in between bites.

He pointed to his cup of coffee. "This is the breakfast of champions." He frowned down at his cup, twirling it around in a circle.

I arched a brow. "So what's really going on, Dad?"

He cleared his throat. "Sin, I found this great job out in Arizona." He smiled stiffly. "It's a promotion with more money. I can't pass up this opportunity."

Just like that, I lost my appetite. I slammed my fork down before pushing away my plate.

"I'm not moving again, Dad. When I started high school, you promised we wouldn't move again."

His mouth tightened. "Things change."

I crossed my arms. "Well, I'm not moving. I'm happy here. For the first time in my life, I have a best friend and a potential boyfriend."

"This is not debatable, Sin. I delayed this as long as I could. We're moving at the end of the month."

"At the end of the month?" I swallowed around the lump in my throat. "I like him, Dad, and he actually likes me too."

He sighed. "Sin, don't make this more difficult than it already is. We're moving."

I flinched. "I'm going to be late for school." Standing stiffly, I grabbed my backpack and tossed it over my shoulder.

"This conversation isn't over, young lady." He crossed his arms. "After school, you'll come straight home."

My eyes widened. "No, I'm not. I'm going out with Kyle for my birthday."

He stood up. "Sin, you live in my house, so you'll abide by my rules."

My fists clenched and unclenched. "I hate you."

The color drained from this face. "Like I said, my house, my damn rules."

"Whatever," I said before storming out of the kitchen.

I didn't give a shit about what he'd said or what he wanted. And I was determined to show him I was no longer his little girl.

After school, I disobeyed my dad and went out with Kyle.

After hanging out with him all night and coming in after curfew, I went home to find a cop car pulling away. Racing up the front stairs, I slammed into the house to find Grace sitting on the stairs with a drink in her hand, reeking of alcohol.

"Why were the cops here?" I asked, my heart pounding.

"Where the hell were you?" Grace slurred as she wobbled to her feet. "Where's Dad?"

Grace ignored me while she straightened her disheveled clothing. "Grace?"

"He went out looking for you." Guzzling her drink, she looked at me with bloodshot eyes that lacked focus. "A car slammed into his, sending him off the bridge. He's...dead."

Tears streamed down my face. Lurching forward, I sought her comfort for once in my life. Grace sloshed her drink, warding me off. With a flushed face, she tightened her mouth before she turned on her heel and staggered up the stairs.

Jade's voice jerked me out of the past. "Sin? Are you okay?"

"I miss him so damn much." Tears filled my eyes, making me feel like that broken girl once again. I wiped away my teardrops, hating I was still racked with so much guilt and self-loathing about that day.

Instead of telling him, *I hate you*, I wished all I had said was, *I love you, Dad.*

She walked toward me with her arms wide open. "Come here."

I swatted her arms, but she pulled me into a hug anyway. I quickly hugged her before stepping back.

Her eyes softened. "Let it go. Forgive yourself and remember how much he loved you." She stepped forward, smoothing my hair. "Honor his love for you and wear the bracelet."

It was time to let go of the guilt. I couldn't bring him back, and pretending I didn't miss him almost every day was disrespectful to his memory. "Yeah, you're right," I said. "You know you're the bestest friend ever?"

She sidled up beside me, hip checking me. "Yes, I am, and don't you forget it."

I yanked her hair before strolling out of the kitchen and through the living room with her on my heels. Stopping in my guest bedroom, I went to the pile of fabric stacked on top of the trunk. Pushing aside the folded remnants, I stared at the old, worn trunk that used to be my father's. Running my fingers along the aged leather, I smiled. Dad had dragged the ratty trunk around the country to every place we moved. The scratched surface was so worn and dirty that I couldn't tell the original color.

Unlatching the lock, I lifted the top. Pulling out a stack of photos and sorting through them, I blinked when I saw one of Dad and me, taken on the beach. He was smiling, and I was sticking out my tongue at the camera.

I missed him. I fucking missed him every day.

How abruptly I had lost him hurt. It had changed me, leaving me vulnerable and scared to let any new people into my life for fear of losing them.

"Sin?"

I cleared my throat. "God, I haven't seen this stuff in years," I muttered, continuing to sift through the photos. I stopped at a photo of a blond-haired version of myself hugging Jade.

She snatched the photo. "Ew, it's blond Sin. Promise me you'll never ever dye your hair again."

"You don't have to worry about that," I mumbled. I dug into the bottom of the trunk before pulling out the small silk bundle containing the bracelet. Unwrapping the fabric, I saw the impressive agate silver piece was still in excellent condition. I ran my fingers along the stones set into the silver. Holding it up, I examined each of the panels in between the stones, hand-engraved with patterns from scrolls to flowers to cross-hatching plaids. Turning it over to the backside, I noticed the small, very faint but readable lettering, "To my love Aubrey." It was strange that this was the first time I'd actually noticed the engraving. *Who is Aubrey? My Scottish great-grandmother?* For some strange reason, Dad never talked about his family, only saying that he had no family left. After clasping the bracelet around my wrist, I started to close the trunk, when something odd caught my eye.

I blinked and then blinked again. "What's this?"

I yanked at the piece of red leather peeking out of the

broken bottom of the trunk. No, it wasn't broken. I hit the bottom. With the thump of my palm, a secret compartment shifted completely, and a plume of dust rose, revealing a well-worn leather ledger.

"What is that?" Jade asked impatiently, looking up from admiring the photos.

"Some weird journal was buried in the bottom of my dad's trunk." I lifted the cover and flipped through the thin paper. It crackled against my fingertips.

"What's in it? Dirty secrets?" Jade asked.

The first several pages were a collection of names. This was not my father's handwriting. The initials G.L.C. were scrawled in red ink at the bottom of every page. Next came numbers and phone numbers. All the pages had codes running along the margins.

"Nothing I understand."

The ledger had been deliberately concealed in the false bottom. *Why did Dad hide this?*

My dad had been the most transparent person I knew, and if he'd hidden it, there had to be a good reason.

I pushed the journal back into the false bottom, banged the base back into place, and then dumped everything I'd pulled out back on top of it, promising myself to further investigate the ledger over the weekend.

❧ 7 ❧

SINTHIA

Jade and I walked out of my townhouse and down the stairs toward Kirby, Jade's chauffeur.

He was leaning against the expensive luxury SUV. He pushed away, tilting his head toward us. "You look lovely, Miss Michaels."

"Thank you, Kirby." I smiled impishly at him. "How's my favorite man?"

He smiled. "Still way too old for you."

I winked at him. "Age is nothing but a number."

I loved messing with Kirby. He was an older version of James Bond—gray but still hot and dangerous.

Jade rolled her eyes. "Will you get in?"

He chuckled while opening the door, and then he helped us maneuver our gowns into the SUV. He strolled around to the driver's side and slid in while we fastened our seat belts.

Kirby fastened his own seat belt before turning the key and revving the engine. He smoothly pulled into the Manhattan traffic before zipping in and out of the snarl of taxicabs and buses.

Jade pulled out her cell, pressing her cheek against mine. "Selfie time," she chirped. "Smile, Sin." She pouted prettily.

I scowled. "Nothing to smile about," I responded dryly.

"Got it." She took the photo. "And posted." She kissed my cheek. "And next time, you'd better smile because I assure you that grimace will be torn apart by my followers." She threw the cell in her clutch.

"Nice. More critics. That's exactly what I need right now." I rubbed my temple, feeling a wicked headache approaching. "Why am I doing this again?" I mumbled under my breath while frowning at the gridlocked New York City traffic.

She leaned her head on my shoulder. "Because there's a special place in hell for people who don't support their besties."

"I hate these types of events with rich people parading down the red carpet like racehorses."

"Hey"—she gave me a fake pout—"rich person here."

I petted her silky black hair like a horse's mane. "And you're my favorite rich person," I cooed.

"So rude." Jade swatted my hand.

I laughed. "Come on. You know what I mean. I hate these things. Red carpets are so fucking intimidating," I explained. "Not that the paparazzi will be remotely interested in me, but I do have to walk down the thing in order to get into the gala." I winked at her. "And more importantly, the open bar."

"The red carpet is scary, even for me, but you can do this." She squeezed my hand reassuringly. "I've seen you give a lecture on fashion design in front of hundreds of sarcastic, know-it-all young fashion students. You can do this." She leaned forward and tapped on Kirby's shoulder. "Don't you agree?"

"Miss Michaels is tough as nails." Kirby winked at me in the rearview mirror.

All too soon, we slowed, and I could see flickers of light up the road. We were in line to be dropped off. Kirby pulled up to the venue and stopped.

I stared at the flashing cameras in shock. "Why the hell do you do this?"

I sat there, stuck, trying to get mentally prepared to step

out in front of the paparazzi's cameras. It was sensory overload. The bright side of this whole fiasco was the media coverage I would get from the Bellisarios wearing my couture gowns tonight.

Kirby got out of the SUV, opened the door, and helped Jade out.

"Jade! Jade!" the paparazzi screamed.

Jade was undoubtedly one of Hollywood's most beautiful actresses, and the media was obsessed with her glam style and beauty. But I knew she was more than just good looks. She was genuine and smart.

Kirby reached for me.

I took a deep breath and hesitated. "Well, all righty, time to make tonight my bitch," I grumbled.

Kirby smiled at me, and I grabbed his hand. I put on my I-don't-give-a-shit face as I stepped out of the SUV. I wasn't as comfortable as Jade standing in front of hundreds of photographers, so I had to go somewhere else in my mind and pretend I was a confident person in front of a horde of people.

When my feet hit the carpet, the lights exploded everywhere. I lifted the train of my gown and tried to walk around Jade.

The paparazzi screamed questions, coming at me from all directions.

"Sinthia Michaels! Can you pose for a photo?"

"Are you wearing a gown from your upcoming collection?"

"Can you comment on the rumors that you and Core McKay are now business partners?"

I looked at Jade uncomfortably before trying to hurry up the stairs.

"Go, go, go!" the paparazzi said, actually moving to chase me.

Jade wrapped an arm around my waist and whispered, "Relax."

"This is new. I didn't realize I was a celebrity," I muttered.

I plastered a frozen smile on my face as we posed for photos.

"Enjoy it, sweetheart. You deserve it." She stepped aside, allowing me to have additional photos taken by myself.

The flashing lights started to freak me out. I sighed gratefully when Jade looped an arm through mine, leading me away from the cameras.

We ascended the red-carpeted staircase lined with camera crews, photographers, reporters, and other gawkers. Tonight's gala was a tribute to all the wealthy A-listers congregating at the venue.

I surveyed the scene upon entering the mansion. A giant chandelier made from hundreds of red and white roses hung conspicuously above the information desk. The desk was completely covered with red roses rising five feet high.

Jade and I handed over our invitations for inspection, and then we waited patiently while a white-gloved security staffer politely scanned our bodies with a handheld metal detector.

Walking farther into the mansion, we strolled up the main staircase bordered by walls covered in pristine white roses. At the top of the staircase, Cate and Bigsby stood regally as if they were a royal couple and greeted arriving guests. Millions of dollars were at stake tonight, money that could be added to Bigsby's political war chest by wealthy patrons. Cate had corralled and badgered donors to death. No one said no to her unless they wanted to feel her wrath. She was a ruthless, conniving bitch who would think nothing about taking down the most powerful people unless they played nice. All those traits made her an excellent match for Bigsby.

Bigsby adjusted his bow tie, looking ultra-sharp in his black tuxedo with a white silk cummerbund. He advanced forward, offering his hand to me. "Sinthia, it's great to see you."

I shook his hand. Bigsby lingered a second or so too long on the handshake. I quickly pulled my hand away, barely suppressing the urge to wipe my palm on my gown to remove any trace of his touch.

Cate swayed frontward. Her mask of neutrality slipped as she eyed the deep-V neckline plunging to my belly button. Her lips pressed into a thin line. Then she said, "Thank you for coming, Sinthia."

My irritation swelled. Cate was an uptight, judgmental witch. I was at ease with who I was. It had taken me too many years to get comfortable in my skin.

My gaze swept over her gown. It wasn't my design, but I could admit Cate oozed glamour, from her elegant updo to her white-and-black couture ball gown and the pair of white gloves she'd donned.

"I was dragged here," I responded stiffly, nodding over at Jade, "by your arm-twisting niece."

Cate inclined her head with her eyes locked on Jade. "You're late," she snapped.

Jade's lips pursed. "I'm not in the mood to argue tonight. Just be happy I came to this circus."

They faced off tensely.

Cate's eyes narrowed, disapproval turning down the corners of her mouth. She bit out, "Jade, a minute in private." She smiled warmly at Bigsby. "Darling, I'll just be right back." She turned on her heel, walking toward the corner of the room.

Jade swiveled to me and said, "Sin, I'll be right back," and then she followed Cate.

The top of the staircase opened to a huge space. My eyes flickered over the room. The stunning venue had been transformed for the occasion with light-gray sofas and flowers placed throughout. It was amazing and hard to take in the splendor all at once. My gaze paused on Erika and Ariana, who were huddled together and whispering while giving the guests sly glances.

"What a beautiful bracelet. Where did you get it?"

My head snapped to look at Bigsby, only to find his eyes locked on my wrist.

"A gift." I kept my answer short.

"Scottish?"

I arched a brow. "What?"

A muscle twitched beneath Bigsby's left eye. "The bracelet is Victorian Scottish."

"How do you know that?"

Bigsby held up his hand, displaying a chunky gold ruby-and-diamond-encrusted horseshoe ring on his middle finger. "I have a distinct taste for jewelry."

I eyed him suspiciously. He tried to look innocent but failed. I absolutely didn't like something about Bigsby, and my dislike had grown when he launched a bid for New York City mayor as an independent candidate.

"We have something in common—Scottish family roots." His eyes narrowed. "But curiously, your last name isn't Scottish. Why is that?"

I was just about to tell him it was none of his fucking business when a couple I recognized from television sauntered up to him. Bigsby's body tightened as he ran his hand over his salt-and-pepper hair in agitation.

"We'll definitely continue this conversation later." He reached to touch my elbow.

I stepped back, avoiding his caress. His eyes went cold before turning away, promptly dismissing me to greet the couple.

I turned and made a beeline toward Ariana and Erika.

Ariana kissed my cheek before twirling around in the Swarovski crystal-covered halter jersey column dress I had designed. "Go ahead. Tell me how hot I look."

"Ariana, you look beautiful, but trouble is on the horizon, and I need you to rescue my bestie." I pointed my finger over to the corner where Cate had Jade hemmed in while jabbing her bony finger in Jade's face. "Like, right now."

Ariana's face turned thunderous. "I'll be right back," she said before charging over to Cate and Jade.

I smiled at Erika. "So how do you feel in your first Sin Michaels design?"

Erika was stunning. The dark richness of her skin contrasted beautifully against the formfitting pale-yellow silk gown that featured a neckline composed of silver crystal embroidery.

She air-kissed me. "Gorgeous, sexy, perfect. All of the above."

"Good. That's what I like to hear"—I pursed my lips dramatically—"because I'm really sensitive about my shit."

I wasn't kidding. I'd dealt with difficult clients who rejected all my sketches, asked me to try other options, and then ended up picking the first sketch I'd shown them, wasting my precious time. But Erika was the opposite of all my notoriously difficult clients. When I'd shown her several sketches, she'd loved them all. She'd said she wouldn't pick, and she'd wear whatever I designed for her. That had shocked the shit out of me. I'd been in design heaven when she gave me complete creative control.

Erika looped an arm through mine. We walked toward the thick of the gala patrons milling around. "My husband has been drooling over me, and that's worth the price of admission, darling." She grinned at me. "Oh, speak of the handsome devil."

A tall blond man walked over to us and kissed Erika's cheek with a twinkle in his eyes.

"Darling, this is Sinthia, the designer I told you about. Sinthia, this is my husband, Mitch Fillion."

I never met Mitch while dating Kyle. I noted he looked nothing like Kyle, except for his blond hair.

Mitch stepped forward and shook my hand. "Erika was talking about you nonstop on the limo ride over here." He smiled at Erika. "It takes a lot to impress my wife."

Erika leaned forward and whispered, "I've got a girl crush."

He chuckled. "Should I be worried?"

She smiled up at him. "Nope. My girl-on-girl phase disintegrated when I graduated from college. I'm all yours."

I could tell they were in love.

Mitch wrapped his arm around her. "After our energetic limo action, I'm not complaining." He kissed her ear.

I almost swallowed my tongue when the Television Producer

Voted Most Likely to Bitch-Slap an Actor giggled like a damn schoolgirl.

Erika pinched his ass.

I cleared my throat loudly and said, "Right here, guys. I'm right here."

Normally, couple PDA made me uncomfortable, but they were cute.

Erika inclined her head, peering around the room, when her eyes narrowed. I turned to look at what had caught her eye. It was Kyle and a blonde barreling through the crowd toward us.

My breathing picked up. I was baffled as to why I had a lump in my throat while my stomach churned. Maybe it was because I hadn't seen him since the night I caught him cheating. The heartbreaking memory of his jeans bunched around his ankles and a blonde preparing to deep-throat him hit me. Kyle had ripped my heart out and stomped on it until it was a bloody pulp. Yet, here he was, heading for me with a ridiculously big smile on his handsome face, staring at me as if we were long-lost friends. As abruptly as the feelings had appeared, they disappeared.

"Mitch, you'd better do something." Erika's heated stare bore into Mitch. "I swear if he says anything to embarrass Sinthia, I'll castrate him."

Erika's vehemence broke the tension, and I bit back a laugh. I could tell Erika wasn't bluffing from the way her fingers clenched and unclenched as if she were actually squeezing the shit out of Kyle's balls.

"Calm down, Erika." Mitch patted her arm. "He won't. I warned him I wouldn't tolerate his rude behavior." He looked at me. "Sinthia, Erika didn't go into detail, but she did make it very clear that Kyle was less than kind to you in high school." He sighed heavily. "The long and short of it is I wasn't the greatest father when his mother and I were married. Kyle went through a rebellious asshole phase, and I pretended not to notice."

I smiled, liking his brutal honesty.

He touched my elbow. "I can't make amends for anything he's done in the past, but I can hold him accountable for his behavior tonight. Trust me on this."

"It's okay, Mitch. I'm fine." Surprisingly, I was. There was no pang of unrequited love. There was nothing—no emotions, no desire. Just fucking nothing for Kyle.

Kyle dragged along the beautiful blond woman clinging to him like arm candy. "Sinthia, wow. It's so good to see you," he said, leering at me as if he wanted to eat me alive. "You look really great!"

The blonde's fingers tightened possessively around his arm. Frankly, she was captivatingly beautiful, so I had no idea why she would be insecure in my presence.

I coolly eyed him. "Kyle," I responded.

I really wished I could laugh at the fact that time had not been good to Kyle, but that was far from the truth. He looked the same. Tall and blond, he was gorgeous, with a cocksure smirk that made me want to smack him senseless.

Erika growled, "Oh, for fuck's sake, Kyle, stop staring at Sinthia with your mouth hanging open. Introduce your *wife*." Her hands went to her hips, accentuating her small waist.

"Oh, Kyle." Mitch covered his face with his hand.

He shot Mitch an annoyed stare before looking back to me. "Sin, this is—"

I cut him off. "It's Sinthia, not Sin. Only friends call me Sin."

His smile slipped. "Sinthia, this is my wife, Claire," he muttered under his breath.

I nodded at her politely. She nodded right back.

Thankfully, Jade materialized by my side, looping her arm around mine. "I'm sure you'll be happy to know my family crisis was averted, and no Bellisario was killed in the making of the reality show starring Cate." She turned to smile at Erika and Mitch. "Hello, guys." She pursed her lips at Kyle. "Oh, look, it's Kyle, the prick."

Kyle glared at her, and she glared right back.

A giggle slipped out of Claire's mouth before she slapped a hand over it. Kyle looked at her coolly, and her face went back to a blank mask.

Shit, she was like some marionette being manipulated by her puppet master.

Jade smiled widely at Mitch and Erika. "We'll see you two later. There's a bar calling our names."

I barely had time to wave good-bye to Erika and Mitch before Jade smoothly maneuvered me away.

I glanced over my shoulder to see Kyle leering at me. From the determined glint in his eyes, I knew his mission was to pursue me like a stalker.

"Damn, that was fucking uncomfortable," I whispered.

"He's an idiot. I swear, he was sporting a hard-on while he was drooling over you."

Seeing Kyle again had been that heart-stopping moment I'd dreaded for years. Frankly, it hadn't had quite the drama and anxiety I'd anticipated. I'd felt absolutely nothing—no pitter-patter of my heart, no I-wish-he-were-mine-again angst. I said a thankful prayer to the universe that the conceited, egotistical douchebag was someone else's problem.

"Let's head to the bar. I'm going to need something stronger than champagne to get through this shit of a night," I said.

We strolled amiably among the glittering, star-studded men and women as we each casually snagged a glass of whiskey and a canapé from the passing waiters. Celebrities preened for the photographer floating through the crowd.

Shrewdly, Cate had ensured that only her richest friends were invited, and every one of them was competing for social media clicks and likes. The conversations were punctuated with, "Oh," "Hey," and, "Sorry," as heels landed on long skirts.

Attending enough of these events had taught me how to move in a roomful of vultures. I snickered when men's eyes followed me with blatant interest and their dates clutched on to them tensely while shooting daggers at me. My tattoo-covered back and stripper strut ensured I didn't blend with the affluent crowd, even in my couture gown.

Reaching the venue's midpoint, I glanced across the room, only to see McKay holding court with Ram by the bar. My eyes locked with McKay's, and then the crowd shifted, cutting off our view of each other.

"Damn. Shit just got real," I muttered under my breath.

The throng moved again. McKay was checking me out with unveiled interest.

I tried to calm my beating heart to no avail. Biting my bottom lip, I drank him in. *Jesus.* He looked smoking hot. If you looked up *fuckable* in the dictionary, McKay's photo would be right there next to it. He sizzled in a shawl-collared tuxedo paired with a crisp tailored white shirt, black silk bow tie, black leather shoes, and a Panerai watch. Ram was looking flawless in a white tuxedo. It was masculinity at its finest.

McKay's eyes flashed as he arched his eyebrow at me. I stopped and turned so I was facing Jade and my back was toward McKay.

Jade looked at me curiously. "What's up?"

"Don't look. That's McKay by the bar," I hissed.

Of course, Jade did the exact opposite of what I'd asked and stared boldly in his direction.

I wanted to choke her. "Really? What part of 'don't look' was unclear?"

Staring over my shoulder, Jade whispered loudly, "Which one?"

"In the black tux with the black silk bow tie. He's staring at me like I owe him money," I responded. "Because I do."

"Damn! Look at that face." Jade blinked and then blinked again. "He's crazy hot."

"No. He's just crazy." I turned back around, glaring at him. Okay, he was hot, but I'd be damned if I acknowledged the way my cunt pulsed under his scrutiny.

He appeared hard, domineering, in control. The disdain in

his eyes as he glared at the spoiled-rich patrons said he didn't like them. He barely tolerated them. At least he and I had that much in common. He just didn't fit into their world despite his ultra-expensive suit and shoes. I could tell he didn't want to by the tattoo etched across his neck. People in this world didn't have tattoos. They looked down their noses at people like him and me. I guessed he and I did have a little in common.

Jade grinned at me. "Oh my! He's definitely a suck-and-swallow situation."

"If you don't lower your voice, I'm going to cunt-punt your skinny ass across this room. Now calm down and act like a lady for once."

"I am a lady—a freaky lady." She winked before eyeballing McKay. "Jesus. He's big all over. I'd bet you he's packing big time."

I swallowed anxiously because I was way too interested in finding out. "I don't doubt it. Damn! He probably has women lining up for a chance to find out."

She arched a brow. "Including you?"

My pulse accelerated at her question. *Yes.* There was no doubt in my mind that he was bound to be my next mistake.

"Not even touching that question, Jade."

A smile curved her lips. "Scared, huh?"

I sighed. "Not in the least. My bad history with men has taught me to stay away from shiny, sharp objects."

She waggled her eyebrows. "Shit. I'd let him cuff me and spank me, and I'd call him Daddy."

An elderly woman looked at Jade with disdain.

Jade eyed her right back. "Move along, lady. Nothing to see here."

I slapped my hands over my mouth to stop the laughter. "I can see you're planning on making trouble tonight."

"What's new? Besides, you need a little trouble in your life." She looked at me knowingly. "Now, let's get back to McKay. His hot sidekick in the white tux looks promising. Who is he?"

I smiled snidely. "His lover."

Completely mystified, she stared at him. "Really?" She twirled her hair. "After arguing with Cate, I don't have the strength for a sexual conversion."

I laughed, shaking my head. "No. It's his business partner, Ram Steele."

Her eyes narrowed with interest. "Fascinating." She looped her arm through mine and pulled. "We must go over and bask in their hotness."

I didn't budge. "Nope. We're not doing that," I said simply.

Jade smiled widely. "Yes, we are." She paused. "But if you want me to make a scene and call them over, I can do that too. It's your choice, sweetness."

I growled. Jade had the finesse of a bull in a china shop. I knew she would take pleasure in making a scene for a multitude of reasons.

"Fine. Let's go."

She looked at me smugly. "I knew you'd see it my way." She pulled me through the crowd toward McKay and Ram.

McKay's eyes traveled from the top of my head down my curvy body. His wolfish glare made me feel like a mouse beneath the bloodthirsty stare of a cat.

"Lick them," Jade muttered.

I almost tripped. "What?"

"Lick your damn lips," she hissed.

I scoffed, raising my chin in a gesture of defiance.

"Do it. He's checking you out, all marauder-like."

And he was checking me out. His smoldering gaze slowly perused my length in a deliberate way. I went breathless right to the pit of my stomach. I didn't understand how he had the power to make me feel excited, giddy, and turned-on all at the same time.

His mouth curved in that secret way that said he knew how much I wanted him.

Damn it. This is not good.

I wanted to walk in the opposite direction, fleeing from his disturbing, heated focus. But McKay was a beast of prey, and any sign of fear would be my doom and his victory.

I sighed with relief when Bigsby ambled over to McKay and said something to him. McKay nodded to Ram before stalking away from the bar with Bigsby at his heels.

Jade stopped, looking at me incredulously. "Where the hell are they going?"

I tried to quash the glimmer of disappointment as I watched McKay navigate through the crowd and up the staircase.

"Hopefully home," I said while grabbing a champagne flute from a passing tray before downing it like water.

❦ *8* ❦

SINTHIA

THE NIGHT WAS TURNING out exactly as I'd envisioned it—boring. Between Kyle stalking me from the perimeter of the room and no sign of McKay, I drank more alcohol than should have been allowed.

It was like a fucking circus. Botoxed and siliconed-to-death women were trying to catch the attention of the hired photographer roaming with a camera around his neck as he playfully snapped shots of celebrities. Cate and her fiancé Bigsby made the rounds. Erika and Mitch meandered about. And I was drinking solo while Jade did her Bellisario duty by circulating among the boring guests.

I had many moments of wanting to pull my hair out from sheer boredom or wanting to leave to get some much-needed sleep. I would have, but I'd promised Jade I would stick it out until the end of the event.

Damn. This night was turning out to be one big epic fail. I thought it couldn't get worse—until I saw Kyle's wife making a beeline toward me.

I sighed loudly. *Let the drama begin.*

"Hello," Claire said, standing in front of me while twitching nervously.

Her designer gown clung to her slender frame. She looked as though she'd blow away if I breathed too hard in her direction. There was one thing for certain. Kyle's wife was drop-dead gorgeous. By her whole aura, I could also tell she was well-bred and came from lots of money.

I arched a brow. "Hello." Nonchalantly, I continued sipping my drink.

I bit back a laugh, fascinated by the antsy flutter of Claire's eyes as they discreetly darted around as if she expected Kyle to fly into a rage at seeing her talking to me.

Her mouth tilted into a brief, small smile. "I love the gown you created for Erika. You have a keen sense of design."

Raising a dark brow, I said, "Thank you."

"This conversation is...awkward, isn't it?" She chewed on her lower lip in consternation.

My lips twisted into a smirk. "Yes, very."

A smile curved her lips. "Exactly."

I shrugged. "But I get it. You're stuck at a gala with your husband's ex. It's natural to be curious."

"When did you two date?" she demanded in a low tone.

I sipped my drink, looking at her pointedly. "He was my high school crush," I responded. I left out the fact that Kyle was my introduction to fucking like horny rabbits in every position and place we could find—his parents' boat, under the high school bleachers, the back of his expensive convertible.

Claire couldn't hide her incredulity. "High school?" she inquired, her eyes wide. "He just seemed so...happy and elated to see you."

I shrugged. "What can I say? I'm an enchanting kind of chick." I kept my tone conversational.

She bit her bottom lip with a worried look in her baby-blue eyes.

"Look, Claire, Kyle and I have been over for years. I have no interest in him whatsoever." I drained my glass.

"Kyle and I have an open marriage." She cleared her throat.

"Well, the open part is something he wants. From the way he's been watching you tonight, I just assumed you and he were sleeping with each other." Confusion clouded her gaze.

Watching? Kyle was eye-fucking me from across the room.

With an aggravated sigh, I said, "Absolutely not. He's not my type." I paused. "Anymore."

"He's rich and handsome. He's everyone's type."

I rolled my eyes. "I don't give a shit what you think, Claire. You came over to me, asking questions, and I'm answering even though I don't fucking have to."

I stared, contemplating where I wanted to go with this conversation since Claire was being very polite. I just couldn't even muster up the strength to be a bitch and dislike her.

"So how did you meet Kyle?"

Years ago, I'd learned that, for some reason, the super-rich loved talking about their personal lives.

"We grew up together," she offered tentatively.

I scrutinized her. "It figures," I muttered under my breath.

Claire actually smiled. "I know. It's pathetic."

I smiled back. "I'm trying not to judge...too hard."

"I heard Mitch warning him to stay away from you." She frowned. "I was curious because of the way Kyle sounded when mentioning your name." She bit her bottom lip, looking at me apologetically. "So I asked around about you." She eyed me sheepishly.

I stiffened. "Invading my privacy? That's a pretty fucked-up thing to do."

She held up her hand. "I'm sorry, but I had to know."

I frowned. "Had to know what?"

"Who my competition is."

There it is. The claws are finally out.

I laughed, looking her up and down with disdain. "Sweetie, from where I'm standing, there is no competition."

She licked her lips. "You're taking this the wrong way. I'm not trying to fight. I'm telling you to stay away from my husband."

I frowned. "Shouldn't you be telling your husband to stay away from me?"

"I have."

I shrugged. "Okay. Well, problem solved. Are we done?"

She stared at me tensely.

I sighed loudly. "What makes you think Kyle's interested in me?"

Her mouth tightened. "Because you're exactly his type."

I choked and then cleared my throat loudly. *No, she didn't say I was Kyle's type.* "That's funny because when he broke up with me, he made it abundantly clear I could never be his type." It was a fact that still stung to this day.

She tapped her glass anxiously, but the look in her eyes was icy and conniving. "I didn't mean to upset you, Sinthia. I just—"

I blinked. *What's up with this passive-aggressive bitch?*

One minute, Claire had been timid and nervous, and the next, she was ready to rip out my throat.

I cut her off. "For the last time, I'm not interested in fucking your husband." I placed my glass on the bar. I was so done with this conversation.

"Sinthia, I'm really sorry for..." Claire blinked as if she were ready to cry.

Bullshit. She wasn't sorry. She was a manipulative wench, putting on a show to garner sympathy from the guests, acting like I was a whore who was trying to steal her husband.

Not giving her a chance to finish, I pinned her under a hard look. "Nice meeting you, Claire," I said before calmly walking away.

"Bitch," Claire mumbled.

"I heard that," I responded without bothering to turn around. Weaving through the crowd, I stopped a passing waiter. "Where's access to the rooftop?" I needed air and space to get away from the bullshit.

He pointed to the spiral staircase. "Top of the stairs and toward the left."

"Thanks," I responded before making my way up the grand staircase to the top floor.

I froze when I felt something brush against my ass. Whirling around so fast, I almost stumbled down the stairs before firm hands gripped and steadied me. They were Kyle's. The idiot was holding on to me with a fucking stupid look on his face.

I pulled away from him, stepping securely onto the landing. "Did you just touch my ass?" I snapped, pointing in his face.

He stepped closer, spreading his hand across my hip. I promptly knocked it off.

"I couldn't help myself. Damn, you are so tempting."

I refused to let him intimidate me. With my chin tilted stubbornly, I held my ground. "Touch me again, and I will fuck you up. I don't care who's watching, including your wife," I said, my voice flat.

He held up his hands in front of him in fake surrender. "Whoa." He laughed. "I'm not a fighter. I'm a lover."

I was done with his stupid ass. "Why are you stalking me, Kyle?"

"Seeing you stirred up old memories"—he licked his lips and studied me—"like memories of how good we were together in bed."

I scoffed. "First, you're married. Second, you're fucking married," I said with a sneer.

"My wife and I have an understanding. I'm free to see and sleep with whomever I want."

"What you're suggesting is—"

His lips twisted into a mockery of a smile. "A no-strings, no-promises night of hot, sweaty sex." His voice held a cocky confidence.

I scrunched up my nose. He was truly a worthless piece of shit.

I pasted a smile on my face and delivered my next line in a saccharine tone. "I wouldn't fuck you even if you had a thousand-dollar bill stuck to your limp cock."

His smile slipped. "Liar," he accused. "I saw the way you were staring at me."

The dude was fucking delusional. I couldn't believe I'd let him steal my chances for a normal relationship with every single guy I met after him. Well, no more. He wasn't worth it.

I balled up my fist, stepping toward him. "That was a gaze of disgust. Get a damn clue, Kyle."

"Are you seeing someone?"

I scrutinized him as if he'd lost his mind.

"You didn't answer, so that means no." He grinned like he'd won the fucking lottery.

My nostrils flared. "I didn't answer because it's none of your fucking business, Kyle."

I wasn't about to divulge that I hadn't had someone in my life for years. Yes, I'd occasionally had sex with a man when I missed the sensual touch of a lover, but I hadn't formed any relationships. I was too emotionally detached for that.

"We can make this work, Sinthia."

"Fuck off." I smiled icily.

Rage twisted Kyle's face, but just for an instant. Turning on my heel, I walked away.

"This is far from over, Sinthia. I'll be seeing you." His dark tone rang with deadly promise.

"Not if I see you first, idiot," I said in a singsong voice, swaying with a grin. There was nothing better than closing the book on an asshole ex.

I veered off to the left, only to see two hulking men leaning on each side of the entryway to the rooftop. I watched Bigsby as he exited the rooftop, storming past the men guarding it.

Shit. He's heading my way.

I'd avoided the prick all night. I wasn't about to have a long, boring conversation that involved him leering at me like some sex object. I dipped into the empty ladies' restroom and waited for him to walk past it. I could hear his footsteps approaching the restroom. Then they stopped, and he walked away.

Taking an extra precaution, I waited a beat before stepping out. I breathed a sigh of relief that Bigsby was gone, but the two men were still standing guard at the entrance. Biting my bottom lip, I debated whether I wanted to mess with the two MMA-looking men or just go back downstairs to the gala. Without a doubt, I knew either Bigsby or Kyle would be waiting to pounce as soon as I stepped into the party. I sighed. That left only one choice—onward toward the rooftop. I swayed down the hallway, stopping before the two men leaning up against the wall with their thick arms crossed. Each one was built like a fucking tank and each just shy of six feet tall.

I smiled winningly at them. "Is the President of the United States out there on the rooftop?"

They didn't crack a smile.

Wow. Tough crowd.

"As gorgeous"—I winked at them—"and intimidating as you two obviously are, I'm going to have to ask you both to get the fuck out of my way. I need fresh air and lots of it. So if the president isn't out there, having some kind of clandestine meeting about saving the world, then I'm going to the rooftop."

I stepped forward, and they swiftly closed ranks. Irritated, I tried to push them out of the way, but it was like pushing a brick wall.

"Whoa. Now, hang on a minute, sweet cheeks," said the one with sandy hair, holding his palms out to ward me off.

I impishly swayed back and forth. "Come on now. Are you really going to make me kick your ass in my pretty dress?"

They both grinned before the one with sandy hair, looking strong as an ox, said, "Sorry. Not going to be able to let you on the rooftop, sugar."

I surged forward again. "Bullshit. I'm not just going to stand here."

The one with sandy hair widened his stance.

"Move out of my way."

The other man with a blond buzz cut and a maniacal glint in

his eyes said, "It's reserved, but come back later, and I'll arrange something real private."

He gave me an adorably rakish grin, and his eyes flicked to mine flirtatiously. I bit back a smile. He was hot, but I wasn't interested.

"Private? With you?" I pursed my lips. "Not going to happen." I crossed my arms over my chest. "Move," I huffed impatiently.

A deep voice rumbled from the rooftop. "Let her through."

They cleared the entrance, allowing me to walk to the lighted rooftop with its medieval architecture and vines hugging the bricks.

I skidded to a stop when one of them said, "Wicked tattoos, sugar."

I turned around to find them both staring at me with sly grins.

The one with the buzz cut winked at me.

"I give him two weeks," the one with sandy hair said to the other one.

They stepped back to flank the entrance.

Two weeks for what?

I turned around to find Core McKay staring at me with no smile. He was standing under the bright moonlight, looking delicious, dangerous, and just plain fucking gorgeous.

"Making trouble everywhere you go," he drawled in that ridiculously gruff tone.

My cunt clenched like it recognized its master's voice.

"What can I say? I'm a very bad girl." I batted my eyelashes almost comically before sashaying toward him.

Stopping before him, I tilted my head, and my eyes traveled up his tall, well-built body. He had discarded the tuxedo jacket he wore earlier. Muscles bunched against his white shirt, and his rolled-up sleeves displayed the tattoos on his forearms. His collar was unbuttoned, and all I could focus on was the all-seeing eye tattoo on his neck.

Damn. This didn't bode well for me. I was a sucker for men with tattoos.

He crossed his muscular arms. "Hmm...that happens to be my favorite type of woman."

He was sexy—well, hot and scary. His dark hair was cut short on the sides, but it was stylishly longer on top. His searing steel-gray eyes made me visualize seriously wicked, naughty things.

Shit. Shit. Shit. Sin, focus.

As the cool air whirled around us, I sauntered past him to take in the beautiful views of both downtown and uptown Manhattan as well as the Hudson River.

Feeling his intense gaze, I sighed before turning and leaning a hip against the ornate railing. I glared coolly at him. Nothing about him was pretty-boy like or classically handsome. He was just very attractive in a rugged and dangerous way.

He regarded me for a long time before smoothing a hand across his blunt-cut midnight-black hair. And just like that, he smiled an actual bad-boy smirk that made my pulse race and sex clench as I imagined all the sexy, kinky possibilities.

McKay was lethal. I shook my head, feeling possessed by his presence. With one look, the man could turn my brain into mush every single time.

"So I heard Kyle Fillion is following you around like a lost puppy. Are you two fucking?" McKay asked boldly.

"Not even close." I sighed heavily. "We dated in high school. He was a fuck-repeat-and-fuck-again fling."

His eyes flashed as he arched his eyebrow at me. "High school?" His lips twitched into a mockery of a smile. "He's chasing you around like you two fucked yesterday. That shit is pathetic."

I tilted my head, kind of enjoying the sarcastic ruthlessness of McKay's demeanor. "What can I say? Obviously, what's between my legs is really memorable."

McKay laughed, and it was a full-on sexy sound, which sent a zing to my cunt.

"Apparently." He eyed me silently.

I squared my shoulders and took a deep breath. "Why are you gawking at me like that?"

He shrugged one massive shoulder. "Just trying to figure you out."

I knew he was toying with me, but I was in no mood for games.

"There's no riddle to me, McKay."

"I beg to differ." His lips tilted into a brief, small smile.

I pasted a smile on my face and delivered my next line in a saccharine tone. "So are you going to continue to eye-fuck me?"

"Maybe."

He smirked, and my heart skipped a beat.

I started to fidget, and then I forced myself to stand still. This man was fucking unnerving.

McKay reached up to run his fingers over my hair.

My jaw dropped. "McKay."

Ignoring me, he expertly pulled my hair from its updo, sending the strands cascading around my shoulders. "You should always wear your hair down," he said simply.

In seconds, I'd gone from wanting to claw his eyes out to full-blown lust. *Damn.* I wanted to let him touch me and screw me in ways I'd let no other man before.

He reached out, grazing the side of my cheek with the back of his hand. "It makes you look...sinful."

My clit pulsed, and my knees nearly buckled from the sultriness of his voice.

I cleared my throat. "Well, this has been...interesting." *And fucking scary.* "Nice seeing you, McKay," I mumbled, stepping forward to make a hasty exit.

McKay placed a possessive hand on my hip, and my body froze.

"I didn't dismiss you," he said with a hard voice.

I pressed my lips into a thin line. "I don't need permission, McKay." I looked down pointedly at his hand. "You want that?"

He spread his fingers across my hip, firmly guiding me to him. His eyes lingered on my lips. "Yes. More than I should."

I swallowed hard. Everything that had come out of his mouth was served with a hot side of dirty sex.

"I'm still not interested."

He bent down close. "Liar," he breathed huskily in my ear, his mouth skirting around the lobe.

"I don't mix sex and business." I pursed my lips. "And more importantly, I don't like you."

He edged forward slightly, squeezing my hip. "Another lie." He pulled away from my ear and winked at me. "Besides, what does liking me have to do with us fucking?" He actually smirked as if he found me mildly amusing. "Angry sex is the best type of fucking, sweetness."

I swatted his hand. "Behave, McKay."

His muscular arm encircled my waist, bringing our upper bodies together. His hand threaded through my long hair. "I don't know shit about behaving."

I struggled to break his embrace. "Don't," I said shakily.

He held my face while staring at me intently. "Why are you afraid of me?"

"Let go of me," I snapped.

He released his hold—not because I'd asked him to, but because he wanted to. Gathering my composure, I walked away, and then I stopped, turning to stare at him. I knew I should have kept going, but it wasn't in my nature to tuck my tail and run, even when it was in my best interest.

"Just for the record, I'm not afraid of you, McKay."

His confident smile called me a liar.

I was done with the cloak-and-dagger routine and decided to lay my cards on the table. "I'm cautious about your motivation. Nothing about you is straightforward. Everything is smoke and mirrors." With my heart pumping, I was raring for a fight. "Yes, I'm attracted to you, but it doesn't mean I'm going to rip off my panties and yell, 'Come and get it.' You're going to have to work fucking hard for that shit to happen."

McKay leveled his gaze on me.

I resumed. "You're an arrogant prick. I get it. You're a sexier-than-thou chick magnet, but it doesn't mean you have to be so cold about our business quagmire either."

He arched a brow. "Meaning?"

"One, you hung up on me yesterday, all rude-like. Two, you keep flexing your muscles as though I'm your minion."

The vein along his jaw pulsed. "Exactly what do you want from me, Sinthia?"

My fists tightened. "I want out of our contract."

His eyes were blazing, and he pressed his lips into a thin line. It was a look of fury I'd never seen on his face before.

"Try again," he said.

I refused to let him intimidate me. With my chin angled stubbornly, I held my ground. "Everything is negotiable, so let's negotiate."

Raising a black brow, he stated, "You have nothing to negotiate with."

I sensed his anger simmering just below the surface.

"I'm the talent and the designer, so I have plenty to negotiate with. If I walk, you're left with nothing."

"I call bullshit on that threat. You'd never walk."

Damn, he called me on my bluff.

I turned my head, unable to meet his taunting gray gaze.

He continued. "And if you do, I won't even think twice about destroying your ass and taking everything you have, including your name. Next."

Fucking asshole.

I forced myself to look at him again. "Next, what?"

"What else are you willing to negotiate with?" He looked me up and down sensually.

My breath caught in my throat as I blinked hard. "Not going to happen. I'm not a whore."

86

"Never said you were."

I closed my eyes tightly to block the sight of his hateful presence. "You didn't have to say shit. That crazy, wild look in your eyes says it all, McKay."

"I make you uneasy," he stated matter-of-factly.

I opened my eyes. *Hell yes.* "Not even close," I lied.

He was the only man I'd met who could make me jumpy like some high school virgin, and I didn't know why. I knew men. I collected them like trophies and threw them away, but McKay wasn't a man I could play with like a Ken doll and toss aside. He was the motherfucking rugged and raw real deal. I couldn't manipulate him with the flutter of my eyelashes, and that made me fucking uncomfortable.

He gave me a calculating look. "Come here." He kept his voice low and soft but left no room to doubt that he'd issued a command.

I placed my fingers on my hips. "I'm not a dog. Don't bark at me like that."

McKay watched me with those devastating gray eyes, his expression giving away nothing. "If you're scared, it's understandable." He widened his stance. "But I don't bite."

An image of me stripped down with him nipping and biting my inner thighs flashed through my head. He smiled as if he knew exactly what I was thinking.

"Unless you enjoy getting bitten." His lips twisted into a smirk. "Then I'm so down with that, darling."

Between clenched teeth, I said, "Why does everything that comes out of your mouth sound so scandalous and dirty?" I bit my bottom lip. "You're nothing like those stiff, smelly old moneybags downstairs."

He stiffened.

No. He was nothing like them. He was an enigma I needed to solve in order to get the upper hand. Even after scouring the internet for additional information I could use as leverage against him, I'd found nothing—no photos, no scandals. I'd only discovered speculation and gossip about his alleged ties to the criminal world—his billion-dollar empire having been built using drug trafficking, money laundering, prostitution, and a few other criminally speculated trades. The only bit of information that did pop up over and over was his ownership of the McKay Club, a chain of private invite-only clubs that were essentially playgrounds for the powerful, rich, and kinky to indulge in discreet liaisons to allow all their freaky fantasies to come true.

"Because I'm not. I've earned my money the hard way, darling."

I scrunched up my nose. "Yes, I've heard. Crime—the unpretty, messy side of Core McKay."

"I'm not afraid to get my hands dirty, Sinthia," he spoke with quiet menace. "That's the big difference between me and all those pretty people downstairs. I fucking earned every dime I have. No one gave me shit. There was no trust fund, no job at some fucking law firm, no Ivy League college. I grew up on the streets, and what I am is nothing compared to those elitist pricks down there. I'm better." He smiled. "You're better. And don't let that attorney boy, Kyle Fillion, make you think otherwise."

Against my better judgment, I walked toward him. "I don't care about him or anyone else." I licked my bottom lip. "I am who I am. Anyone who can't accept me can kiss my ass," I finished, standing before him.

"And just for the record—" he leaned down, and his tongue swirled over the delicate folds of my ear "—I'd love to kiss and lick every inch of your beautiful ass."

Holy shit. My breath came more raggedly. My nipples tightened, and warmth pooled between my thighs. What I wouldn't give to ride him hard and fast.

He trailed a thick finger across my collarbone. My heartbeat pounded in my chest. My knees almost buckled when he pushed down my dress strap. He brushed a hand against my breast, and my nipples stiffened immediately.

The sensations of his touch, his clean, masculine scent mingling with the crisp air, and the heat emanating from his body made me heady. He arched down, and his breath skittered along my shoulder before his tongue traced the scar running across it. Losing all sense of self-preservation, I reached up and ran my fingers along the back of his head, sinking my nails into the silky softness of his hair with my fingers splayed against his scalp. I closed my eyes, bowing into him. Our embrace was oddly sensual and too comforting.

This wasn't right. My eyes opened. Breaking the surreal moment, I released my grip on his head and swallowed nervously. Abruptly, his head snapped up, and gray eyes locked on to mine.

Tracing a callused digit over my scar, he asked, "What happened?"

Feeling a little self-conscious, I gave him a stiff smile. "I ran into a stalker with a knife. He won round one. He's gone. I'm here. So it's over." At least, I hoped it was.

McKay frowned as he snaked an arm around my waist, pulling me flush against him. "If it's not, let me know. I can take care of him for you." The smooth proffer of violence in his sophisticated tone was a cold reminder that underneath his expensive tuxedo was a deadly predator.

"Thanks, but I can take care of myself."

The way he looked at me told me he begged to differ. I pulled away, straightening my dress. I didn't need him to run my personal life. No man was going to come in and save the day.

"What you think is going to happen between us will not happen," I said calmly.

He caught my chin, and his gaze bored into mine. "It already has."

His words sent a shiver through me, but I smiled and tried to make light of my surging emotions. "You wouldn't know what to do with me, McKay, because I guarantee you, I'm nothing like any woman you've ever met." I was broken and cranky, but right now, I was also confused and horny.

I gasped when he wrapped my hair around his powerful wrist, tugging my head back so our lips almost but not quite touched.

"You mean a woman who hides behind her pain with snarls and quips?"

I tried to pull back, but my hair was still tightly wound about his wrist. He continued to hold me.

"Let me go, McKay."

He ignored my request and said, "I can see the pain behind your eyes. Let me help you unlock it."

It took several moments before I could compose myself enough to reply. "You don't know shit about me."

"Liar. You're like an open book to me." He nipped my bottom lip. "And when you're ready to get on your knees and beg me to fuck you hard and dirty, I'm going to read you from cover to cover."

In seconds, I'd gone from anger to arousal. I wanted him to touch and fuck me in ways I'd only dreamed about. Then I knew. I was no match for him. He would consume me, fuck me, and spit me out without a backward glance.

He whispered against my lips, "And I have a lot of dirty little things planned for you, Sinthia."

My pulse accelerated. My fingers curled and fisted the fabric of his crisp white shirt. His physical magnetism was palpable. I swallowed hard, trying to resist the urge to lick the all-seeing eye tattoo on the side of his neck.

"I want to strip you naked and lay you on my bed." There was a pause before he said, "I want to tie your legs wide open, so I can see your glistening cunt." His voice was low and rough when he growled, "I will work you with my tongue until you're begging and screaming."

It was so easy to imagine his tongue lapping my womanhood with desire that a deep shiver shook my body.

I tried to get away from his grasp, but he held me close.

"Then I will kiss you." He cradled the back of my head, easing my mouth to his. The kiss was slow, methodical, and scorching hot. He drew my bottom lip into his mouth, sucking softly, until my insides were quivering with need.

He eased back, and his bright gray eyes searched my face. He gave me one last swipe of his tongue before he bit my lower lip and retreated. "Letting you taste yourself on my lips."

The truth of McKay's pull irritated me to no end. Everything about him was overpowering. His touch, voice, and mere presence demanded surrender—my surrender. It was as if he'd known his dirty talk would be my kryptonite.

"I never mix business and sex," I said with way more bravado than I actually felt. "It would just create a wickedly bad scene when I decide to dump your ass."

With any man, it would, but McKay wouldn't give me a second thought. That was the part that made it so humbling.

"Tough words." He reached up to run his fingers over my hair, rubbing a strand between his thumb and forefinger. "That only confirms that you want to fuck me just as badly as I want to fuck you." Steel laced his tone.

"What can I say? I could never resist a man with a big dick and swagger," I responded before reluctantly stepping out of his grip, "until today."

His face twitched. I pinched back the urge to caress the faint jagged scar running across his eyebrow. At that moment, I knew McKay would be my undoing. No matter how hard I fought the inevitable, I would end up right where he wanted—in his bed.

"I see right through you, McKay, and I have no interest in being the fucktoy you'll discard when you get bored."

He narrowed his eyes. "Maybe you see right through me because we have a lot in common." He reached down, trailing a finger along my scar. "Like the fact that neither one of us gives a shit about attachments." He leaned downward, kissing my scar. "Sounds like a match made in heaven," he mumbled against my skin.

I reached to push his head away, but somehow, my fingers decided to make a home in his thick hair.

In a sadistic way, he was right. He and I were an ideal match. We didn't give a shit about relationships or playing house. We had an itch, and we both needed to scratch it. But something in the back of my mind warned me that going down this road with McKay would be disastrous for me emotionally.

From my past mistakes, I'd learned to pay heed to my inner voice. And this smoldering lust between us was already out of control. I was playing with fire, and I knew it. He was a strictly do-not-touch proposition, yet I was dancing near the flames, enjoying the fire as it burned my cheeks.

Any chance of disguising my need was shot to hell when he trailed his finger across the cleavage displayed by my low-cut dress. Splaying his hand across my breast, he flicked open the beaded hook holding my dress closed with his thumb.

My full breasts spilled out. Immediately, my hands went to jerk it shut.

"Don't," he ordered, his voice low and rough.

I dropped my hands. Strangely, everything about this man made me want to please and obey.

A smile curved his lips. My heart skipped a beat as I tried to remember how to breathe. He covered my breast with his big hand, moving his palm back and forth over my bare skin.

Willing my mind to function, I stared up at him, blinking. "Oh God," I breathed. My breasts felt swollen. Desire coiled low in my belly, causing my insides to spasm with need.

"I can't wait to fuck you and make you mine."

"I can't do this, McKay." But I wanted to.

"You will—sooner rather than later. It's inevitable," McKay said, never taking his eyes off me for a second. "And when you do, I'm going balls deep in you."

I swallowed hard and bit my bottom lip to hide the emotion that had it trembling. It was too easy to imagine being naked with him, and my pussy flexed in anticipation.

His nostrils flared, and every muscle in his body seemed to tense, straining against his shirt. "But only if you say please." In one smooth motion, McKay released me. He eased back, and his steel-gray eyes searched my face.

Still reeling from McKay's erotic words, I couldn't wrap my brain around losing myself to him. My hands shook while fastening the front of my gown closed.

This was the first time in my life I was scared to death—not of him, but of how out of control his mere presence made me feel. The dirty, naughty things he made me want to do, like fall to my knees and deep-throat him right here in the open.

Not giving me a chance to recover, he pinned me under a hard look. "Go, Sinthia, before I change my mind and order you to get on your knees and suck me dry." There was hardness in his soft words, daring me to disobey his order.

I raised my chin in a gesture of defiance and met his gaze. "Good-bye, McKay," I muttered under my breath before turning on my heel. I walked away, ignoring the hole he was likely boring into my back with his gaze. And like a coward, I picked up speed and ran off the rooftop.

❧ 9 ❧

CORE

IGNORING MAX'S and Rocco's knowing stares, I paced back and forth on the rooftop.

Sinthia Michaels was trouble, and she was just my type of woman. Now all I could think about was fucking her so hard she would taste my cock in the back of her throat.

Shit. How the hell did I let it go so far?

I'd known I was fucked when I watched her strolling into the gala. Her body moved like a panther—sexy, determined, and confident. She was tall and voluptuous with curves that cried out to be caressed. In a matter of minutes, she'd shattered my control. It had taken every bit of self-restraint not to back her into a dark corner, pull up her dress, and fuck the shit out of her.

I'd been obsessed with her bombshell body since our meeting at my office. She was one of the most stunning women I'd laid eyes on. I'd memorized her every feature from her rich, olive-colored skin, bow-shaped full lips, and tilted nose. Her long hair cascaded around her shoulders like a sheet of fine silk. It was all confirmation that I was losing sight of my goal to use Sinthia to get to Bigsby. I'd had to remind myself several times that she was just a pawn to be played to trap him.

But when she'd swayed onto the rooftop, I'd seen the fire and determination in her eyes, and my cock had gotten hard.

Damn. I loved it.

Not many women or men had the nerve to go toe-to-toe with me. It was a shame Sinthia and I hadn't met under different circumstances, but I was playing to win. And Bigsby Calhoune was my game.

Max looked at me hesitantly. "Core? Are you ready to go, bro?"

"I'll meet you two downstairs. I need a minute to cool off."

"I bet you do," Rocco mumbled.

Max and Rocco nodded, and then they turned and left.

I clenched and unclenched my hands by my sides as I took a deep breath. My body was on edge with the need to find Sinthia and finish what we'd started. I was aroused at the mere thought. I couldn't remember the last time I'd wanted someone with the intensity I felt for Sinthia, but I knew I'd have to get over it fast.

My mind raced out of control. *Why the fuck did I have to meet her under such fucked-up circumstances?*

Running my hand through my hair, I stopped short and then slammed my fist against the wall.

Fuck it.

I'd wanted to bend her over the balcony rail and shove my cock so far up her cunt that I wouldn't know where she ended and I began.

It didn't help matters that she was exactly the type of woman I was attracted to.

Shit, she'd looked fucking gorgeous when she welcomed my touch. Her beautiful hazel eyes had glazed over with lust. Her full, pouty lips had turned up at the corners as if begging me to delve further. It was sensual the way her face had glowed, and more importantly, her body had reacted to my touch like a woman tuned to my fingers. All the while, her head had tipped to the side as if taunting me to break her, to make her beg.

Little had she known that her lack of submission was like

waving a red flag in front of a bull. My sadistic streak had pushed to the forefront with the burning urge to make Sinthia mine—well, at least temporarily. Eventually, I would tire of her, as I had with all women. My life wasn't conducive to any attachments, even a momentary one.

My lips curved up. It hadn't even bothered me when Mitch told me she'd called him about helping her break our contract. Mitch had thought I would be angry, but it was quite the opposite. I loved a woman who was willing to fight, willing to get her hands dirty, because that was what it would take to stand against me. Going against me was like bringing a knife to a gunfight. It would be a bloody slaughter. I would crush her to get what I wanted, and I wouldn't lose a bit of sleep about it.

I was ruthless, cold, and sadistic. That was how my enemies had described me. But I hadn't gone from street thug to self-made international business mogul by making friends and kissing asses. I did what was necessary. What most people couldn't or shouldn't, I would do that and more. That was how I had accomplished about ninety-nine percent of the things I'd done in my life, and Sinthia Michaels wasn't going to be an exception.

I waited for the inevitable. *What will be her next move? Will she offer her body in exchange for getting out of the contract?* No. She didn't seem like that type of woman. Besides, that wouldn't work. I'd just fuck her and still crush her. But I loved a challenge.

I'd been tempted to tell Mitch to take her on as a client. It would be fun to play around with her like a cat with a mouse, but that would be a waste of my time and hers. Our agreement was ironclad. But, damn, just anticipating her next move was fun. I had no doubt she would continue trying to wiggle her way out of our contract.

Ram came strolling up to me. "So what did Bigsby say?"

"What?" I asked in a low tone.

In exasperation, he threw his arms up in the air. "What the fuck is wrong with you?"

"Nothing." I shot him an irritated stare. "He did a song and dance, apologizing for his behavior toward me at his fundraiser a couple weeks ago."

I shrugged, but it still irked me, remembering how the asshole's eyes had scrutinized the tattoo on my neck. He had clearly not approved of my presence at his dinner event until Mitch had admonished him by pointing out I was Core McKay —as in McKay Corporation, one of Mitch's biggest clients.

"But I knew he was trying to feel me out about the Sin Michaels deal. He'll be calling me soon. I guarantee you." Bigsby was a pompous asshole, and I had no mercy for idiots. My nostrils flared. "We'll wait for his next move. I saw the desperation in his eyes. It won't be long. Trust me."

As if shit couldn't get worse, dipshit Kyle Fillion appeared on the rooftop, decked out in his preppy designer tuxedo. His carefully coiffed blond hair gleamed, and his face was tanned and clean-shaven. I could practically smell the money on him as he walked up to Ram and me.

"Hey, Core. Have you seen a gorgeous brunette with a beautiful ass on the rooftop?" he asked, fixing me with a toothpaste-ad grin.

My fingers curled into fists as I struggled to hold on to my temper. "Excuse me?" I asked, taking a menacing step forward.

I despised Kyle. He was the kind of snob who used to look down on me when I'd been just a poor kid from the projects with a single mom who worked hard by stripping to put food on the table. I was far from poor now, but I'd never forget how it'd felt to be treated like dirt by guys like him.

Kyle ran a hand through his hair. "Sinthia Michaels. Bigsby said he saw her up here." He grinned. "Damn! I can't believe how good she looks. If I'd known she would turn out so hot, I wouldn't have dumped her ass." A wistful expression crossed his face.

I angled my face in a silent warning, never letting my eyes drop from Kyle's. "She's not interested in you," I delivered between clenched teeth, not bothering to hide the fury building within me.

Confusion clouded his gaze. "Wait. Are you fucking her?"

I closed my eyes, trying to bottle the rage bubbling to the surface. I wanted to punch this smug, rich motherfucker in the face and break every damn bone in his body. My eyes snapped open.

He clapped me on the back. "Never mind. It doesn't matter. A woman like her wouldn't think twice about fucking both of us." He winked at me. "I don't mind sharing." A smile curved his lips.

"She's mine," I said to Kyle in a calm but icy tone, grabbing him by the throat. I rammed him against the wall effortlessly, ignoring his yelp of outrage.

"How dare you touch me!" Kyle screeched. He tried to get away from my grasp, but I held him close. "I'll fucking sue you."

"You must have a death wish, Kyle." Anger coursed through my veins as I squeezed.

Kyle sputtered and clawed. The more he struggled, the tighter I constricted. The urge to extinguish his worthless life burned like a fire through my blood until I felt strong hands trying to pull me off of him.

"Core? What the hell?" Ram barked.

I released Kyle.

"Are you insane! I'll..." Kyle huffed and puffed as he quickly tried to straighten his jacket.

My temper and general take-no-shit attitude were known far and wide among both my enemies and peers. I had no damn clue why Kyle hadn't gotten the message.

"You'll what?" I scowled, stepping forward and leveling an ice-cold glower at him. "You want to dance, big boy?" I hissed.

Kyle gave Ram a stricken look. "Ram, this is bullshit. He's out of control."

"Don't fucking look at Ram. Look at me, you sniveling

wimp." My tone demanded attention. "He can't fucking protect you. I'm the one you should be worried about."

Kyle dusted off his tuxedo jacket. "I'm not afraid of you, Core."

I stepped into his space, staring him down. "You should be." Cold dismissal hung off every word. I shoved him away. "Now get the fuck out of my face," I spoke with quiet menace.

He held up his hand before storming off.

"What's wrong with you?" Ram asked in a careful tone. His eyes widened. "Fuck! Sinthia Michaels? Are you actually thinking about tapping that ass?"

"And what if I was?" My irritation swelled. I really didn't want to talk about this shit.

"She's hot. I get it." Ram shook his head, annoyance etched on every line of his face. "But you can't fuck her, Core, for multiple reasons. Most importantly, it would be fucking messy."

"What if I don't give a shit about messy?" Challenge dripped off the words.

Common sense told me to walk away from this clusterfuck. That had been my plan until I walked into the gala and she looked at me with that bad-girl stare mixed with a side of trouble. There wasn't anything contrived about the sway of her hips as she'd walked toward me with an impish smile. It had been wicked and real, which said she wasn't the type to run from several rounds of hard fucking.

Ram actually shook his head, and disapproval turned down the corners of his mouth. "Core, don't do this. You're thinking with your fucking cock."

I leveled him with a glare. "I don't need a lecture from you, Ram. I got this."

With a snort, he cut his hand through the air. "I give up. Have it your way."

I rolled my shoulders. "I always do," I snapped before striding past him.

I would be damned if I admitted Ram was right. This was

the first time in my life that I was thinking with my cock like some oversexed teenager.

Basic, raw hunger surged through me, beating at my self-control. Sinthia was everything I wanted in a woman—strong and feisty. I was becoming painfully hard. The idea of fighting to have Sinthia submit to me had my cock throbbing and my balls aching. *Damn.* I had no doubt she'd battle me like a hellcat, and I couldn't wait to find out how hard she'd fight.

❅   10   ❅

CORE

INFURIATED by my encounter at the gala with Sinthia, I plopped down on my bed. The playful, curvaceous woman always seemed to be one step ahead. Her tenacity made me crave her even more. My attraction to her was trouble and distracting.

I had to stay focused on the mission—the destruction of Bigsby Calhoune. Tucking my hands behind my head, I thought back to the night Bigsby had changed my life by killing my mother.

~

MANHATTAN. TWENTY-SIX YEARS AGO

MOM GRABBED MY CHIN. "LOOK AT THAT MUG." SHE SHOOK HER head, dark red hair swirling around her. "What did I tell you about fighting?" She eyed the bruises and cuts on my face.

I pulled away. "Leave me alone." Lowering my head, I waited for her to leave. When I didn't hear the sound of her retreating feet, I roared, "They called you a whore!" I tried to keep the bitterness from seeping into my voice, but as I thought of her stripping in front of drunken men night after night, I found the task even more difficult with each passing moment.

She gasped, her mouth opening and then shutting, as if she couldn't believe what she was hearing. "Core, I dance for a living to put food on the table. I don't give a shit what those snotty-nosed boys from the neighborhood think." She stared at me. "Do you?"

I shook my head, but I did. By now, I should have been used to hearing the horrible names the kids from the building called her, but it hurt as bad as it had the first time. "I hate it here. Why can't we move?" I despised everything about living in our cramped one-bedroom apartment in the crime-ridden, drug-infested project—from the pungent aromas of fish and burned meat that wafted through the air to the piles of garbage lining the dirty sidewalks.

She sighed heavily. "I'm working on it, baby. Real soon I'll have the money to move us out of here. We'll have a fresh start." She ruffled my hair. "You'll see."

I knew she was trying to make a better life for us. Nothing had been easy for her while raising me alone. I despised the fact that my biological father had abandoned us, leaving her before I was born. All I'd ever been told was that he and Mom had a one-night stand, and he'd wanted Mom to have an abortion. When she'd backed out at the last minute, he dumped her and told her he didn't want anything to do with me.

"You promise?" I asked.

She beamed, brushing my hair away from my forehead. "I promise, baby." The doorbell rang, and her face tensed. "That's my friend. He's going to help me with my money problem. I'll be right back."

I frowned. "What friend?"

Mom didn't have any friends. She'd said the women from work were too catty and manipulative.

"That's none of your business, Core. Just stay in your room and do your homework, okay?"

"Okay," I responded grudgingly. She walked through the bedroom door, and I cracked open my math book, dreading doing my homework. When I heard my mother's bloodcurdling scream, adrenaline coursed through my veins, and I ran out of my bedroom, through the living room,

into the kitchen, where I saw her being pinned against the wall by a huge, burly man whose back was facing me.

My hands trembled as I watched helplessly in horror while the man repeatedly beat her face to a pulp.

"I warned you to keep your big fucking mouth shut, but you didn't listen," the man rasped. "Now you're going to end up like Cruickshank —dead."

Mom struggled to breathe. "Please. I'm sorry. I promise. I won't say anything."

"It's too late for begging," the man said with menace while punching her face.

I charged, jumping onto the man's back while trying to claw his eyes out of his head.

I could still hear the bone-crunching thud Mom's frail body made as the man slammed her to the floor.

The man swung around and yelled at me, "You little bastard, you're dead!" He grabbed me by the neck before throwing me clear across the kitchen.

My head smashed against the corner of the kitchen counter before my body bounced onto the floor.

Dazed, I slowly reached my hand up to my head. I felt the oozing thickness of gushing blood across my eyebrow, but I refused to give in to the pain. Mom needed me.

My heart had leaped out of my chest when my mother screamed, "Leave my son alone, you fucking bastard. This is between you and me, damn coward."

The man charged at her, pulling a .357 Magnum from his beltline. "Shut the fuck up, whore. You brought this on yourself. I warned you to keep your damn mouth shut!" he yelled while grabbing her by the hair with one hand.

Turning her face away from him, the man placed the gun to her head. It seemed like an eternity to me as I stared at the gold ruby-and-diamond–encrusted horseshoe ring on the man's middle finger before he fired the gun, killing Mom. He then stormed over to me with his gun aimed toward me before squeezing off some rounds, and then my world went completely dark.

~

MANHATTAN. PRESENT DAY

I JERKED STRAIGHT UP IN BED, DRENCHED IN SWEAT AND MY heart racing. The nightmares every night were the first clue that something wasn't right with my recollection of Mom's death. Events of that mind-numbing night replayed in excruciating detail like a horrible horror movie, revealing details I'd long forgotten.

Running my hands through my hair, I swung my legs over the bed. I leaned forward, putting my elbows on my knees and my face in my hands. There were too many pieces to the puzzle, and none of them fit together perfectly. I couldn't shake the feeling that I was overlooking a key connection between Bigsby and Mom's death.

Sighing, I sat up, scrubbing my hands over my face. I stood, deciding against taking a shower. I needed to burn off some frustration in my home gym this morning. I put on sweats and a T-shirt, and I went downstairs to find the morning ritual of the team gathering in my kitchen for breakfast in full swing.

Immediately going to the coffeepot, I grumbled under my breath, "Just one damn morning to myself—that's all I fucking ask."

Despite the fact that each team member had his own luxury apartment, it never failed that command central was always my penthouse. I didn't know how, but over the years, our living quarters had turned into a quasi-fraternity house with the one elevator giving us unlimited access to each other's spaces. It was a good thing none of us had a special woman in our lives. God knew no woman would be able to cope with the lack of privacy due to the team running through our penthouses unannounced.

I poured a cup of coffee before glancing around the kitchen again, taking stock of my team. Ram was at my kitchen table, frowning into his coffee mug. Max was shoveling bacon and eggs into his mouth like he hadn't eaten in days. Rocco was cooking while jamming to some hard rock pouring from his tablet. Kevin was pacing back and forth with his cell pressed against his ear.

Even with the lack of solitude, these four men were my family, closer than flesh and blood. I'd take a bullet for any one of them, and I knew they'd do the same for me.

There was Ram, of course—my best friend and partner. Then Max and Rocco, brothers and my enforcers, handled all my dirty work. They'd knock the heads that needed knocking together, roughing up all my enemies and keeping my business associates in line—not because I forced them to do it, but because the sick bastards loved the hell out of inflicting blood and carnage. Kevin took care of the financing and accounting for all my businesses. He was also a tech genius with connections to people in high and low places, making him a highly skilled intelligence asset. Everyone played their part. For years, we'd tightened up my operations along the East Coast, making us all filthy rich because of it.

We'd all made hard sacrifices to get to where we were today, including loving and losing people we'd cared about. Losing the love of my life, Maya, had cut me deep, sending me to a dark and wild place. I'd sunk into the abyss of violence and crime, abandoning Maya's and my dream of leaving the criminal world behind and starting anew.

Only Ram's friendship had pulled me back from the brink of despair and death. We'd focused on a way to go legit. Real estate had been the fastest way out. We hadn't been fazed by the fact that the close-knit world of real estate wasn't about to let thugs like us through the doors. So we'd used bribes, violence, and our connections in the criminal world to fuel our ascent. When we'd broken ground on our first building, I'd known it was just a prelude to the legitimate money to come, fulfilling Maya's dream.

I smiled. She would be so proud of me if she were still alive. Many people underestimated me, but she hadn't. I'd beaten the odds by working long, hard hours to build my empire from the ground up. What I hadn't known about real estate, I'd figured out through trial and error. Now I was part owner of a multibillion-dollar real estate development and investment company with offices in New York and Miami, including a portfolio of condo projects, hotels, and office buildings.

I stared at Ram. "Rough night?"

Ram looked up and nodded.

Max bit off a piece of bacon savagely. "Yeah, right. After the gala, he was banging the shit out of that socialite chick, Cate Bellisario."

I smirked. "Did she tell you anything we can use against Bigsby?"

We were ruthless. I didn't mind taking a hell of a lot of pride in that.

Ram stood up and stretched. "How could she? She had my cock down her throat for half the night." He groaned, walking toward the refrigerator. "I'd thought I was into some freaky shit, but damn, the weird shit she begged me to do to her made me a little uncomfortable." He pulled out a bottle of water and then leveled me with a glare. "The things I do for the job."

Rocco looked over his shoulder and snorted. "Poor baby. Fucking a hot chick is just such sweaty, hard work."

Ram punched him in the shoulder. "Shut the fuck up."

I leaned against the granite countertop, gulping my coffee. "I didn't tell you to fuck her. I said to use her obsession with you to get more leverage on Bigsby."

"You know me." Ram grinned as he twisted open the bottle. "I don't mind going real deep in the name of work."

My lips tilted into a brief, small smile. "I bet you don't," I replied.

Max and Rocco chuckled.

Cate was a frequent patron at the McKay Club. She had a seedy dark side she kept well hidden from her fiancé Bigsby. I'd known, with a little nudge from Ram, Cate would jump at the chance to fuck him. She was our ace in the hole. It would be just a matter of time before she was so strung out on Ram that she would do or say anything to keep getting fucked.

Kevin talked rapidly into his cell. "Are you sure? Okay... Yes. Keep digging. Talk to you later." His brows knitted, his bewilderment evident, as he strode around the counter, shoving his cell into his pocket. Opening the refrigerator, he grabbed a bottle of water.

"What's on the agenda for today?" Rocco turned from the stove with his plate piled high. He sat down before shoveling food into his mouth.

"We need to work on our leads." I drained my coffee cup and refilled it.

"Which ones?" Max asked.

"All of them," I responded.

Kevin choked on his water. "All of them?"

"Every damn one of them. The trail on Lexis was getting cold, but now that we know Jeff Barolo and Bigsby are linked, we need to work that lead and find out where Jeff's hiding. The Sinthia and Bigsby connection is still hot. We need to work that angle ASAP." I crossed my arms, looking at Kevin as he plopped down. "So what else do we have on him?"

Kevin raked a hand over his face. "Nothing new. I couldn't find any ties between Bigsby and Ben. Are you sure Ben was telling the truth about Bigsby cleaning Ben's money through his company Pomtonic International?"

"Yes," I responded.

Kevin frowned. "I don't have any information verifying that yet. And UF-Star, the independent political action committee spending money to champion Bigsby for mayor, is squeaky-clean."

"And the Jeff Barolo lead?" I asked.

"It's going nowhere. I can't locate him. He's off the fucking grid."

Ram's stoic expression turned grim. "So we have nothing? Why the hell are we paying all this money for intel if you can't produce shit?"

"What the hell is wrong with you? You didn't let me finish," Kevin snapped back.

"Go ahead," Ram responded grudgingly.

Kevin slumped down in his seat. "Bits and pieces of information about Jeff's past are surfacing. He's bad news, and he's had some assault charges. Plus, he's on probation. Eventually, he has to check in with his probation officer. So we've got that covered. The Bigsby and Sinthia angle is dry, and what little information I have, I haven't quite put together, but I will." He crossed his arms.

"What about Sinthia's background? Any skeletons in her closet?" I asked.

"Nothing scandalous. She moved around a lot up until she was seventeen. Her parents seem pretty straitlaced. Her father, Ian Michaels, died years ago in some freak car accident. Her mother, Grace Michaels, owns some overpriced teahouse in Manhattan." Kevin frowned. "But I did find something very interesting. Sinthia has two birth certificates."

I whistled as I rocked back on my heels. "Two? How did you find them?"

"I started with her DMV record." Kevin's voice was calm and easy. "Once I had that, it wasn't hard to trace her birth certificate. I just wasn't counting on finding out she had two."

My lips tightened. "What else did you find?"

"She has two names on record—Sinthia Cruickshank and Sinthia Michaels," Kevin responded.

My shoulders bunched, but I kept my face expressionless. "Cruickshank?" I bit back the expletive hovering on my tongue.

What the hell?

Cruickshank was the person Bigsby had bragged about to Mom.

I started to mention what I knew, but then I stopped. I needed hard information, not remnants from dreams that didn't make a bit of sense. I decided to wait until Kevin could dig up more info before coming to a sound conclusion about what this all meant.

"Yes, Cruickshank," Kevin replied.

Ram inclined his head toward me. "What do you think? Does she know?"

I scowled. "Do I look like a fucking mind reader? I haven't spent enough time feeling her out to know anything concrete about her."

"Oh, you did a hell of a lot of feeling her out," Max said. "I saw the way Sinthia looked after you were done with her on the rooftop. The woman seemed well tousled."

Max and Rocco chuckled.

I shot them a dirty look. "Yeah, okay. Laugh it up, idiots."

Kevin smirked. "What I do know is someone tried real hard to hide her birth certificates, but they weren't counting on the fact that I'm really good at what I do—unearthing shit they'd paid a boatload of money to bury." He smiled smugly. "The first birth certificate has her father listed as Ian Michaels and her mother as Grace Michaels. The second certificate has her father listed as Greer Lorne Cruickshank and her mother as Aubrey Cruickshank."

"Find out if the Cruickshanks are still alive." I rubbed my chin. "Put a tap on Bigsby's cell and follow up with your Fed contacts to see if they know anything about Bigsby. If he's laundering money, he has to be on someone's radar."

Rocco leaned back in his chair, raising a brow. "Okay, I have one word to describe that idea—insane. An unauthorized cell tap on a mayoral candidate?"

My jaw clenched. "So the fuck what?" I countered. "We do that shit all the time." I looked at Kevin. "Just put the tap on." Then I glared at Max. "I need you to put a tail on Sinthia. Follow her discreetly. I want to know everything she does, everywhere she goes, who she interacts with. I even want to know who she's fucking."

Max threw back his head and roared with laughter.

"I told you," Kevin said smoothly, nodding at Ram with a knowing look. "I won the bet. Now pay up, Ram."

Ram threw his arms up in the air in exasperation before taking out his wallet. He pulled out a crisp hundred-dollar bill and slid it over to Kevin.

Kevin picked up the bill before loudly snapping it with a wide smile. "I just love taking your money."

I stiffened. "What bet?"

"I bet Ram you'd crack and order Max to follow her. Ram said you wouldn't," Kevin said, smiling slyly at me.

I couldn't hide my incredulity. "You motherfuckers are taking bets on me? What else are you betting on?"

"How long before you fuck her," Rocco admitted.

Totally deadpan, Max added, "Four thousand dollars on the line, and given how long you and Sinthia were on that rooftop last night, I might just win this bet."

Kevin frowned. "Hey! Why didn't anyone tell me about that bet?"

"Because, Mr. Genius, we knew you'd win," Ram said to Kevin. Then he looked at me. "I can't believe you ordered Max to follow her. Damn it. She's not who you should be following. That should be Bigsby."

"That's for damn sure," Max mumbled as he got up. He put his plate and utensils into the dishwasher.

"Don't tell me what I should be fucking doing. I have millions invested in her. I have a vested interest in keeping tabs on her," I responded coolly.

Ram shook his head. "Bullshit! If you care so much about her company, then give me the okay to contact the other retailers so I can give them the thumbs-up to resume business with her."

My jaw twitched. It'd been a while since I'd wanted to take Ram's head off so badly. "Why do you give a shit?" I asked, not bothering to hide the rage building within me. "You interested in fucking her?" In an instant, my hackles rose as my eyes locked on to Ram accusingly, and I slammed my empty cup on the counter.

Ram's mouth turned up into a smile. "She's hot, but I'm not a blocker. No matter how much you deny it, I know you. You'll be fucking her by the end of the month."

I wanted to deny it. Everything about Sinthia Michaels was complicated, too complicated, but I wanted her in my bed. I knew she wanted to be there too, but for some reason, she was hesitant and damn skittish. I needed time to work her a little more. I wanted no doubts to be in her mind when we fucked.

"Given what I know about her, I'm going to have to take it slow until I figure out what's going on between her and Bigsby," I clipped out.

Leaning up against the wall with his thick arms crossed, Max sent me a you-are-so-full-of-shit look. "Uh-huh. I call bullshit on that, Core."

A smile twitched across Rocco's lips. "Me too. Shit. Every time anyone mentions her name, you get that look, bro."

My irritation swelled. "What look?"

Ram took a large swallow of water before responding, "The look you get when we're about to take over a company—predatory, focused, and possessive."

Ram knew me well. He was right. From the minute Sinthia had stepped onto that rooftop, I'd known it was time for a change, and she would be the woman who could satisfy my distinct and dark sexual tastes. I wanted her despite the fact that there were a million reasons I shouldn't.

It didn't hurt that I loved her point of view about sex and

me, because she pulled no punches. She was a welcome change from both the women who threw themselves at me because of my money and those I slept with to sate my sexual cravings. None of it was real, and all of it was exhausting.

"Are you fucking with me right now?" Kevin stared at us with an incredulous look on his face. "I can't believe you guys are cosigning on Core going cock deep into her. It's illogical." His voice was rough and serious as usual.

Ram's lips curled up into a smile. "Logic has nothing to do with this shit." That faint smile was still on his lips when he pointed his finger at me. "He's in fuck-and-destroy mode. I say let them fuck it out so he can get her out of his system." He looked at me pointedly. "Besides, I kind of like her. Her take-no-shit attitude reminds me a lot of Maya," he said quietly.

Even after all these years, it was still hard to hear her name. "She's nothing like Maya."

No woman could ever compare to Maya. Maya was the first woman who had loved me for me, who had stood by me when I was poor, and who had grounded me when the money started rolling in and I got lost in fast cars and fast cash.

Maya had been my balance, my rock. The major reason I'd decided to turn my back on my criminal empire was for fear of losing her and my unborn child. But I'd lost her anyway, and my world had shattered into a million pieces. Just one tragic moment, and she'd been taken away, leaving me emotionally void.

Ram stared at me knowingly. "If you ask me, I think it's past time to move on." He cocked his brow at me.

I bit back a growl of frustration, wishing my friend would just shut the fuck up. "I didn't ask you," I grated, "so keep your damn opinions to yourself."

He wanted me to let go of the memories of the love of my life as if she'd meant nothing. If it were so easy, I would have done that years ago, but the loss still hurt like a motherfucker.

Ram's brow furrowed. "I'm just keeping it real. You're thirty-six now. It's been fucking years."

Contrary to his belief, time had not healed old wounds for me. It'd only made the loneliness worse. I longed for her to still be here to enjoy the life I'd built, one that had been in the making when she was by my side. When she'd died, I'd gone on a violent rampage, lashing out at everyone around me, including my friends.

Without her, my life was cold, and I wasn't alive.

My body tensed as the recollections of that fateful day echoed through my mind. Those memories of fire engulfing my SUV, taking Maya with it, had haunted me for years. Making matters worse, I'd never found the person responsible for the car bomb.

~

MANHATTAN. THIRTEEN YEARS AGO

MAYA'S HAND CURLED AROUND MINE. HER EYES WERE WIDE AND filled with excitement as I ushered her along the sidewalk toward my waiting SUV.

She stopped, reaching up to grab my face between her hands. "Have I told you how much I love you?"

"Not in the last hour." I bit her lower lip. "Let me hear it." I hugged her.

"I love you, Core." She wrapped her arms around my waist, burying her face in my chest.

I'd never believed in love until I had hers. She was everything I didn't deserve—kind, loving, tough. And she was mine. She was the first person I woke up to every morning, and I wouldn't have it any other way.

"I love you too." I ran my hand through her hair as she peppered me

with kisses. "Don't tempt me, woman, or I'll take you back upstairs and give you round two of slow and steady fucking."

She tipped back her head and smiled at me. "Promises." She paused. "You know I'd rather be upstairs, being fucked by you, than sitting in floor seats at some basketball game." She frowned, biting her lower lip. "Besides, the tickets cost too much."

And that was one of many things I loved about her. She didn't care about the trappings—money, cars, or the lavish lifestyle—that my illegal deeds had brought me. She loved me for me and embraced me for the man I was—hard and broken.

I grabbed her chin. "Nothing is too much for you. You know that."

She was my kind of perfect.

"Stop spoiling me, Core. I don't care about the money or cars. I just want you—" she stepped back and pressed her palm against her round stomach "—and our baby." Her face pinched with pain, and then she smiled.

"Are you okay?" I asked, looking her over anxiously.

"The baby kicked." She kissed me. "You worry too much. If it were up to you, I would be swathed in bubble wrap."

"You're damn right. I need you and my baby safe." I frowned. "There's just too much shit going on right now."

The tension and violence between my team and a rival gang had been ramping up over territory and money. There was no way around it. Someone was going to get hurt. This was more of an incentive for me to leave the criminal world behind.

"I trust you to protect us, Core." Her smile widened. "Oh, the baby kicked again."

She snatched my hand before placing it on her stomach. I rubbed my hand over the swell of her belly and smiled at the answering movement from my little one.

"See? The baby just said, 'Hell yeah, Daddy.'"

I continued to caress her growing stomach with reverence. I thanked my lucky stars that she wanted a family with me. Bending down, I brushed my lips against hers, and she caught her breath.

"How did a beast like me get such a beauty?"

"What can I say? A big cock and a smile get me every time." She winked at me.

I swatted her ass. "Come on, woman. Let's go to the game and get back home so I can thoroughly ravage you."

With our hands clasped together, we strolled down the sidewalk. I opened the SUV's door, allowing her to get in. Closing the door, I walked around to the driver's side and hopped in.

I glanced over at her while putting the keys in the ignition. "Do you have the tickets?"

She rolled her eyes. "Yes."

I arched a brow. She was prone to forgetfulness.

She dug into her handbag and then looked over at me sheepishly. "Shit. No." She shook her head. "I left them on the kitchen table."

I sighed, killing the engine. "Really?"

"Don't give me that look, Core." She crossed her arms. "A girl can get a little distracted when she's getting fucked on top of the kitchen counter."

I lifted a brow. "Did you enjoy it?"

"Immensely." She smiled impishly.

"Well then, the distraction was well worth it." I winked at her. "I'll get the tickets." I kissed her hard on the lips. "You just stay here and look gorgeous."

"Like this?" She licked her glossy lips, a move that always turned me on.

"Perfect." I leaned forward and licked her bottom lip. Pulling back, I yanked the key out of the ignition before sliding out of my seat and shutting the door behind me.

I turned away and headed for the building.

"Uh, Core?"

I glanced back at her.

"It's cold in here." She pouted playfully. "I need the key."

Sliding the apartment key off the ring, I handed her the key ring before hurrying away.

The next instant, I heard an explosion. The force of the blast threw me back. I yelled as I slammed into the sidewalk. My breath rushed out, and shock froze my body.

A crowd was gathering on the street. Dazed, I reached up, feeling blood oozing from the gash across my cheek. My eyes were on the burning SUV—or what was left of it. My heart slammed into my chest, and tears streamed down my cheeks.

Maya and my baby were dead.

~

I KNEW ONE THING FOR CERTAIN. NO WOMAN COULD REPLACE Maya in my heart, not even the smoldering siren Sinthia.

But I did want her in my bed.

I rubbed my chin, wondering how her dark tresses would look arranged against my pillow. My cock grew hard at the notion.

My thoughts were interrupted by Kevin's loud, animated voice.

"Okay, so what happens if she finds out you're using her as a pawn to bring down Bigsby?"

To annoy him, I just stared at him.

"Well?" he asked, perturbed by the silence as he usually was.

"She won't," I said in a voice sharper than I'd meant it to be. The reminder that I was breaking my number one rule of never mixing business with pleasure was fucking with my mind—big-time. My obsession with her was crazy and fucking reckless, but I found myself shaken by my need to possess her.

Kevin scoffed, "There's a high probability she will."

I slid him a withering glare. "If it happens, I'll deal with it." I wasn't worried about Sinthia finding out.

I'm Core McKay, a billionaire, and I'm always in control.

Once I got her into my bed, she wouldn't be leaving until I was thoroughly sated.

"What I'm more concerned about is Bigsby's interest in her." I frowned, remembering the covetous glint in Bigsby's eyes while he'd eye-fucked Sinthia at the gala. "I have a sneaking suspicion Bigsby's interest in Sinthia is more personal than business." A grim smile curled my lips. "And the faster I can get to the bottom of their connection, the sooner I can get Sinthia into my bed." I stared at Kevin. "So, keep digging."

Kevin took one look at my face and then snorted. "How far do you want me to dig?"

My face hardened, and I drew up to my intimidating full height. I asked icily, "How far do the gates of hell go?"

THANK YOU FOR READING **TWISTED LIES 2!**

More Core and Sin goodness continues with **TWISTED LIES 3!**

And sign up for my newsletter to find out about new books...
www.sedonavenez.com/newsletter

ABOUT THE AUTHOR

USA TODAY BESTSELLING AUTHOR SEDONA VENEZ lives in New York City with her hot ex-military hubby—hooah—and their fur babies. She loves writing sizzling, sexy intricate stories about strong but broken characters who push limits, overcome their fears and risk it all for love.

Sedona loves to connect with readers!
www.sedonavenez.com

OTHER TITLES BY SEDONA VENEZ

Aliens!
Galaxy Alien Warriors - The Box Set
Beauty and the Alien Beast

Paranormal Romance
Shifter Alphas Furever Series
Claimed by Her Two Alphas
Claimed by Her Wolf
Claimed by Her Bear
Claimed by Her Dragon

Paranormal Romance
Credence Curse Series
Breaking the Storm
When Lightning Strikes
Taming the Beast
Reason to Love
Taming the Alpha Beast - The Box Set

Werewolves!
Wolf Elite Series

Operation Wolf: Gunner
Operation Wolf: Eli
Operation Wolf: Hunter
Wolf Elite - The Box Set

Bears!
Bear Elite Series
Operation Bear

Dark Romance
Dirty Secrets Series
Twisted Lies
Twisted Lies 2
Twisted Lies 3
Twisted Lies 4
Dirty Secrets - The Box Set

Contemporary Romance (MFM Ménage)
Standalone
Shameless Desires

Billionaire Romance
Standalone
Mr. Billionaire CEO

Urban Fantasy Romance
Magic Fire Collection

EXCERPT: TAMING THE BEAST

Want to sample a new series? Check out my Credence Curse books including this book, <u>Taming the Beast</u>.

I was stark naked—again. With huge ebony breasts swaying, ass jiggling, and designer stiletto-encased feet slapping against the dewy grass, I sauntered over to the center of the clearing.

Perching myself on top of the smooth boulder—or what I now lovingly called my rock of shame—I surveyed my recurring fixation.

My heart seemed to freeze and then pound. "Damn. You're such a beautiful kitty," I whispered.

Water cascaded off the tiger's magnificent reddish-rusty coat with narrow dark-brown stripes as he prowled out of the river toward me with rippling muscles. Its chest, throat, muzzle, and the insides of its limbs were creamy with a milky-colored area above the eyes that spread onto his cheeks.

When I extended my hand, he tilted his large head down, rubbing against it with a chuff-chuff sound.

"Hello, my big kitty. I'm happy to see you again, too," I answered his greeting. My digits trailed up to the white spot present on the back of its ear.

He nudged my hand away before circling me, his fur

caressing my bare legs while I admired the prominent ruff on his head and long tail ringed with noticeable dark bands.

Warmth radiated throughout my body as his fur deliciously tickled me.

"Every dream, you bring me here to watch you swim, and I still don't know why."

My mouth fell open when a deer pranced up to the river and drank from it, completely oblivious to the tiger's presence.

The tiger stilled, waited, and then pounced. The deer didn't even have a chance to run away before the tiger's big-as-saucers paws latched on to its hindquarters, bringing down the deer. The tiger gripped its neck, delivering a crushing bite to its prey. The deer stopped thrashing.

My fingers touched my parted lips before I closed them. "Holy shit."

This was a new addition to my nightly dreams. He'd never killed game before.

Wasting no time, the tiger dragged its dinner toward me, laying the carcass at my feet like an offering.

I gave him a weak half smile, trying desperately not to hurl at the sight of the dead deer. "Thank you, kitty, but it's a little . . . rare for me."

He flicked his tail, making a chuff-chuff sound, before his limbs quivered, shifted, and morphed into a very naked tall, muscular human.

"Elijah?" I stammered.

This couldn't be right. Animals didn't transform into humans, especially not into a man I was crushing on hard in real life.

"Yes, my Hope," he uttered in a dark, masculine voice.

Electricity sparked in my body as my eyes perused his mouthwatering splendor. His short, thick black hair had hints of gold, and his beard was well groomed. But it was his stunning but strange amber eyes with gold flecks that always made my stomach flip-flop, like a fish out of water. His eyes were the windows to his soul. They bored into me with an intensity that made my sex clench.

"Damn. Even in my dream . . . you're fucking splendid," I declared. My eyes trailed down his hard body to his engorged, perfect shaft standing at attention.

He clutched my face between his enormous, calloused hands. "Eyes up here, darling." His face dissolved into an exquisite grin. "Unless you're finally ready to get on all fours for your big kitty?" His hands dropped away and grabbed me around the waist, yanking me against his naked body.

"My, you're such a dirty pussycat, and I love it." I licked his bottom lip.

"So that's a yes." It was a statement, not a question.

"Baby, I'll do whatever you want . . . however you want. But only if you promise to lick all my cream, like a good kitty."

We stared at each other with my legs straddling one of his rock-solid thighs.

"There's nothing good about me, darling, but I can promise to lick you to the very last drop." His voice was thick with emotion. "Just say when, my beautiful mate."

EXCERPT: CLAIMED BY HER TWO ALPHAS

Want to sample a new series? Check out my Shifter Alphas Furever books including this book, <u>Claimed by Her Two Alphas</u>.

In the two weeks since that conversation with Peyton, one snippet of that bizarre conversation kept running through my head. These guys were looking for their perfect *mate*. Not mates, plural. Not one guy wanting one and the other guy wanting... something else. Both guys were looking for the same thing, and according to Alex, that thing was me. But I was only one woman and even if I'd gotten past the weirdness of two guys wanting to share one blind date, I still hadn't wrapped my head around how I could be the perfect mate for both of them.

Yet here I was, trying to figure out how I was going to find not just one, but two blind dates in a crowded bar. I should have backed out.

No. You shouldn't have. It's not going to kill you to do this. If it back-fires, you can tell Peyton "I told you so."

At least I should have figured out some way to recognize these guys, like carrying a rose or wearing a bow in my hair. Or maybe a name tag, so instead of standing in the crowd turning in useless circles, I could find these guys. I made another sweep of the room.

You're overthinking…just take a breath and let go.

I closed my eyes, wavering slightly in my heels, did my best imitation of someone poised and collected, and concentrated on my breathing. Then I opened my eyes. The crowd parted and there he was. Or there *some* guy was, some really handsome guy.

He was sitting at the bar, and he was looking right at me. For a split second I thought I'd made him up, or maybe I'd hallucinated him out of desperation. Even sitting down, he was big and broad-shouldered, taking up more physical space than anyone around him. Or maybe he just looked like he was. He should have been imposing, scary, but he radiated an all-American boy kind of feel, the hunky guy-next-door who helped you with your groceries or changed the flat on your car. *A nice, safe guy.*

Until I got to his eyes. Blue. Even in the dim light of the bar, I could tell they were blue. The all-American hunk had just turned the tiniest bit dangerous. There was a fire in those eyes that woke up something deep and primal, something I'd thought didn't exist in me. Or at least I'd never experienced it. I wouldn't go as far as calling it love at first sight; lust at first sight, maybe. Whatever it was, it was pretty amazing.

I really wanted to take a step forward, but I was rooted in place. His eyes held mine, never looking away, and it was like a magnet, drawing me closer. Something held me back though.

But wait…what about my date? Just because this guy likes looking at me…and I like looking at him…

I turned away, the act of breaking away from his gaze doing nothing to lessen the heat that had built up inside me. I was supposed to be here looking for my mystery men, not falling for the first guy who caught my eye.

Turn around…what if it's him?

That thought came out of the blue. And for once, I listened to the voice in my head and did a slow turn. The guy was smiling at me, and something inside me simultaneously clenched and loosened up. It was a physical sensation, a thud deep and low, and I took a step back, shocked by my body's reaction.

When he stood, I saw just how tall he was, well over six feet. He cut easily through the crowd toward me with a grace that belied his size. He stopped just in front of me, and I looked up into those piercing blue eyes.

"Hi, Sadie. I'm Dane. Dane Hastings."

I stared. Just plain unattractively, open-mouthed, deer-in-headlights stared at this amazing specimen, who'd just told me he was one half of my blind date. Saints preserve me, maybe I'd gotten lucky. Then it hit me.

Where the hell was the other guy?